Jane Doe Mystery, Book 3: Haunted Heart

By Wendy Laing

Writers Exchange E-Publishing

http://www.writers-exchange.com

Jane Doe Mystery, Book 3: Haunted Heart
Copyright 2017, 2024 Wendy Laing
Writers Exchange E-Publishing
PO Box 372
ATHERTON QLD 4883

Cover Art by: Sandy Cummins

Published by Writers Exchange E-Publishing
http://www.writers-exchange.com

Contents

Author's note

Haunted Heart is the third book in the mystery/paranormal series featuring Jane Doe.

This book is set five years on from the second novel *Severance Packages*, to bring it up to a current time frame.

Jane has been happily married to Oliver Tarrant for five years and they live at *Wyndales*, Gisborne.

Detective Chief Inspector Steve Ho is now head of the Special Crime Squad.

Jane has just accepted a new job with promotion to Chief Superintendent as head of the Special Cold Case Unit. Jane labels her first cold case, *Haunted Heart*. It is destined to become one of the most haunting cases in her career.

Again, as the author, I've used settings that I'm familiar with and love within my home state of Victoria, Australia.

Prologue

It was a rather cool Autumn morning. The northerly wind rustled the leaves in the trees near Bridgewater Lake. A young mother and her two children were walking their Labrador dog along the street behind the retirement village, adjacent to the lake and the surrounding gardens. The boy was carrying a plastic bag with some bread scraps from their breakfast, to feed to the lake's two resident white ducks. He ran ahead down the path that lead to the lake and called out, "Hurry up, mum. The ducks are hungry."

His mother, sister and dog caught up with him as he started to toss the bread toward the waddling ducks.

"Save some for your sister to throw."

"Okay, mum. Here's the rest," he replied and handed the bag over to his sister.

Five minutes later the happy family strolled further along the path, and then stopped at a gap in the reeds. The dog paddled out into the water to the length of his extender lead, the water lapping up to his tummy. He tugged further on the lead, nearly pulling the mother into the water.

"Macca, stop! Come back." She tugged on the lead, but he kept straining; his nose pointing a something further out in the lake.

"Macca...come!" she commanded. Her order was ignored. Her son took off his shoes and waded out a short distance to see what the dog was so interested in. He spun around, grabbed the dog's collar and pulled him back to the shore, his face flushed with excitement.

"Mum, there's a man swimming out there!"

She shortened the lead, commanded the dog to "sit and stay," and then handed the lead to her son.

"Wait there, you two, I'll have a look."

She also took off her shoes and went out into the cold water to see for herself. Two minutes later she was back on shore. Pale-faced and with hands trembling, she dialled 000 on her mobile.

"Police? There's a body floating in Bridgewater Lake!"

An hour after the police had met and interviewed the frightened family at the lake; an urgent call came in to Detective Chief Inspector Steve Ho of the special Crime Squad.

"Inspector Ho, it's Senior Sergeant Jason Standing from Broadmeadows CID. We have a body in Bridgewater Lake in Roxburgh Park. But, after identification taken from the body, it looks like a murder case for your squad, Sir."

"What's so special about your body in the lake that needs the attention of our squad?"

"Sir, the wallet on the body indicates that the deceased is Professor Johann de Jong. The death is suspicious. We've deliberately left the body where it is until you get here, Sir."

Ho caught his breath. *Johann de Jong, the eminent transplant surgeon and government consultant! God, his face has been all over the TV news and newspapers the last week. He's been condemning the possible illegal donor organs coming into the country!*

"I'll be right there, Sergeant. In the meantime, I'll alert the chief pathologist that there is a special case coming in." Ho slammed down his phone, and called out, "Charlie? We're wanted out at Roxy urgently!"

"Right, Boss," replied Detective Constable Chan, heaving his tall, burly frame up out of his office chair.

"Ready," responded Detective Sergeant Mary Lamb, as she flicked her frizzy blond hair into a ponytail and then grabbed her shoulder bag. They followed in the slip-stream of Ho, then left the St. Kilda Road headquarters and drove to Roxburgh Park, north of Melbourne.

At the time the body was discovered, Detective Chief Superintendent Jane Doe was walking her two dogs around the paddock at *Wyndales*, in Gisborne. Her mind was relaxed as she watched the two Cavalier King Charles' run gleefully around the short grass.

Heck, I'm beginning to feel nervous about this new job! It's three years since I've been at the pointy end of my job... Don't be stupid, Jane. Pull yourself together, it's another challenge that you need!

"Sassy, Spunky, come! Time for breakfast. Mum's got to go to work today." She smiled as the two brown and white balls of energy flashed past her and headed towards the back verandah, where Oliver was standing waiting for them.

"Hello, my love. You're all just in time. Breakfast is served!" He ushered them in like a proud rooster with his brood.

"Hmm! This looks delicious, Oliver. What would we do without you?" She went inside with him to the kitchen.

"Um...come on Jane, or you'll be late for your new job."

They ate in silence, enjoying the moment of peace before the rush of the working day.

"Got your team organized yet? Or am I not meant to know?"

"Yep! Bluey and Angel. What do you think?" She winked at him.

"Brilliant choice. Bluey Johnson has all the experience you need, and Angela Ho...err...Nguyen...well I'm thrilled she's been promoted to Detective. Does Steve Ho know?

"I told all three yesterday afternoon. Bluey will be a perfect backstop for me, and Angela Nguyen as she is known professionally, is super keen. Her Law/Arts degree will also come in handy. Steve is happy that his wife is working under me. The grandparents are only too happy to act as babysitters to the twins, doing the drop-offs and pick-ups from school."

"Those kids have grown up so quick, Jane."

"Yes! Steve and Angel will be great additions to the team." Jane sipped on her coffee for a few moments in silence, her thoughts in a whirl again.

Lucky things, having children... Stop it Jane, that's water under the bridge. We've got two adorable four-footed kids, and don't forget Oliver, my lovely husband.

She looked over to him and smiled, "What are you doing today?"

"I'm going to have a first contact session with a seven year old girl called Jenny Summers, who is having nightmares about being murdered."

"Hopefully she's not a future clairvoyant! We'll have a lot to talk about tonight over a glass of red." Jane glanced at her watch. "Heck, I'd better go or I'll get delayed by the traffic." She rushed to the bedroom and grabbed her bag, before rushing out into the garage.

Oliver waved as his wife drove past him towards the front gate and disappeared down the road towards the highway to Melbourne.

Day One

Jane drew in a deep breath before she opened the door marked, 'Special Cold Case Squad'.

Come on, Jane, don't be nervous.

She grabbed the door handle and walked in.

"Morning, Ma'am," said Detective Sergeant Stan Johnson, and stood up to attention.

"Hello, Ma'am." Detective Constable Angela Nguyen also moved out of her chair, "Coffee?"

"Morning, gang." Jane smiled, "Firstly, Angel, just call me, Boss, and yes, coffee with milk will be wonderful. Bluey, you can grab two more coffees and that tin of biscuits. We'll need them as I have to go through all the official rigmarole and formalities of the job that we have been selected to do."

Five minutes later, the newly formed 'Special Cold Case Squad' was seated around the large table in the conference room, pens and pads at the ready.

"We won't be the only people working in this office. Obviously, we'll be working in conjunction with police from the regular force in the suburbs, and liaising with the pathology department. As you've no doubt found, this newly renovated office has a special area at the back that looks like a cross between an office and a science lab." Her two staff nodded.

"Well, that's exactly what it is for. Obviously, any autopsies will be conducted at Southbank."

"Will we eventually have a full-time pathologist, Boss?" Stan dropped the biscuit he was dunking and it fell into his cup of coffee, "Crap! Sorry, I'll get a cloth from the kitchenette."

Jane and Angela grinned as he waddled over to the small adjacent room, ran a tap and came back, cloth in hand, his face flushed red.

"Trust me to make a mess on the first day, Boss," he laughed, "My late missus always complained about me leaving stuff on the table."

Jane smiled back at him while he cleaned up the coffee spill.

Good old Stan, we need a bit of life in here...after all, we are going to be dealing with the dead and unsolved mysteries.

"To answer your question, yes, I have someone in mind, but I haven't been able to ask him formally yet. Sorry, but I can't say until it's official." Jane shrugged her shoulders.

"I'm looking forward to this job, Boss," responded Angela, "It'll interesting seeing our special pathologist finding all sorts of things from the dead."

Jane grinned, "The Assistant Commissioner is sorting through some possible cases for us. He wants us to get ourselves organized today and set up files in our filing cabinets and cupboards, our desks. Obviously this unit won't necessarily be toting guns. We're named as the Special Cold Case Squad because we'll be focusing on a high profile case that has either not been solved or needs to be reopened due to the advances in modern pathology techniques, such as DNA. Our results should possibly give closure to some families, and also bring some people to justice." She looked at her watch and stretched. "It's time to get up and move before we fall asleep in here. Bluey, can you start setting up some physical files in our empty filing cabinets and Angel, you can organise getting the contacts of phone numbers of the CID units and Pathology unit, with relevant names ready to be scanned into our mobiles."

"Yes, Boss."

"Files, here I come!" Stan winked.

Jane went to her office to contact her favourite pathologist, and arrange a private chat as soon as possible.

Detective Inspector Steve Ho shook Sergeant Jason Standing's hand. "Hello Jason, this is Detective Sergeant Mary Lamb, and this is Detective Constable Charles Chan."

Standing smiled and visibly relaxed. He had been nervous to meet the famous Steve Ho, who had a fierce reputation in CID. Flicking his greying hair back from his face, he responded, "Sir, I took the liberty of contacting the Assistant Commissioner when I recognised the deceased. I believe Dr Fred Harvey, the chief pathologist, has been asked to do the autopsy on the victim."

"Yes he has, Jason. However, he may not be able to, as I believe he is...err...*was* a very close associate and friend as a fellow academic, of Professor Johann de Jong. Knowing Fred, he'll feel compromised, but I guess we'll see."

The detectives stood over the body of the late Professor Johann de Jong.

"A strong person, Boss," remarked Charlie Chan, "He would have put up a fight and wouldn't have died quietly, but there doesn't appear to be any violence on him."

"Exactly why we think the death is suspicious, Constable," acknowledge Standing.

"Then what the Hell did he die of? I reckon he was dead when he was put in the lake," remarked Mary Lamb, frowning, hands on her hips. "What do you think, Boss?"

Ho nodded, "Yes, Bah Bah, I think you're right. Unfortunately, with all the dog paw marks and the foot prints of the family in the mud here, it might be hard to find any clear evidence of other outside foot prints." Steve looked around him and ran his hand through his jet-black straight hair. "Damn it! Can't blame the locals though for enjoying this lovely area. Alright, Jason, you can let the body go to the morgue. I don't think you'll find much more at this site."

"Yes Sir, but we'll keep looking, just in case."

"Good man. We'll get together after the autopsy has been done, when we can hopefully have some answers as to the cause of death. Then we'll be able to plan tactics to find the killer or killers." Ho shook hands with Standing, smiled and then walked over to Lamb and Chan who were waiting at his car.

"Hello, lovely lady," Doctor Fred Harvey greeted Jane Doe with a hug and a kiss. "Welcome back to the pointy end."

"It's good to be back, Fred. I'll cut straight to the chase as to why I'm here to see you."

"Take a seat, my dear. I'm all ears." Fred Harvey sat down next to Jane on the easy chairs in his office and crossed his legs. Jane was aware of his deep brown eyes staring at her.

She cleared her throat. "I'm here to offer you a new challenge...a new position in my Special Cold Case Squad."

Fred laughed softly and rubbed his grey beard. "I'm not surprised, and the answer is going to be a swift 'Yes!'"

"Hell, that was quick. I thought I'd have to brow-beat you into this job. As you know, it won't be as frantic as your current position as Chief Pathologist, and..."

"Sorry to interrupt you, Jane, but I've been thinking about changing my lifestyle for the past few months. As you no doubt know, I've been on a month's leave, because you've already been talking to the Assistant Chief Commissioner about this position for your squad. Knowing you only too well, you also know it's my first day back here, on the proviso that I let the higher powers know what I want to do...retire... or become a consultant. It's time I slowed down and doing the research and consultant pathology for your unit would suit me down to the ground. End of my speech." He stood up and turned toward her, holding out his hand, "Time to give you a big hug, girl!"

Jane giggled and hugged him. "Thanks mate. When can you start?"

"The sooner, the better...I had a phone call from Steve Ho a couple of hours ago, wanting me to do an autopsy on a body found in a lake in Roxburgh Park, but..."

"You refused?"

He nodded.

"Why?"

"Because the body is a close academic colleague of mine from Melbourne University. I knew I was about to change jobs. Ho's team need to utilise the Central mortuary and pathologists, not me. Between the two of us, I've already had a quick chat with the powers that be in the Attorney General's office and the Assistant Commissioner about my future and advised them that I've been looking for another job or retirement. Strangely enough, the Assistant Commissioner told me there was a perfect position in the offering as a consultant!" He winked at Jane. "So they won't be surprised at the news. His son, Pierre de Jong is identifying him this afternoon."

Jane's jaw dropped. "His father is the infamous Professor Johann de Jong?"

"I'm afraid so. Steve Ho recognised him straight away, but wisely insisted that the son do the formal ID." Fred sighed, and added, "Doctor John Sampson, my now former assistant pathologist, is going to do the deed." Fred grabbed his mobile. "I'd better warn him that I'm becoming a consultant to your squad, and he's about to be in charge. What next?"

"We go to the Assistant Commissioner with our news, and you of course will have to officially notify in writing to your superiors, what you are going to do. You should be able to join us almost straight away."

An hour later, Harvey had made several phone calls and sent out the important emails regarding his new position. The two friends left the Victoria Institute of Forensic Medicine to go to Jane's new office in St. Kilda Road. As Jane drove into the Police Headquarters' car park, she said, "In this situation, I think it will be best for all if you keep your distance from Ho's case. I guess you'll still get lots of feedback from your friends at Southbank, because you'll still be going back and forth to there in your new capacity as our forensic consultant pathologist."

"Yes, of course. It'll be like still working there, but I'm 'freelancing', so to speak, and there won't be the same frantic pressures of my old job, thank goodness."

It was 2 pm by the time Jane Doe and Fred Harvey arrived at the Special Cold Case Unit's new office. They had grabbed some take-away food in the canteen downstairs before heading to the lift in the lobby.

Harvey stood back and ushered her into the lift, "You first, Boss!"

She grinned at him and said, "It's strange hearing you calling me Boss. Please call me Jane. The rest of the team won't mind."

"I look forward to meeting them. Who are they, by the way?"

"Wait and see!"

Jane swung the office door open. "Afternoon gang. Let me introduce Doctor Fred Harvey; former Chief Pathologist, now our very own consultant pathologist! Fred, this is Detective Sergeant Stan Johnson, and this is Detective Constable Angela Nguyen."

Fred chuckled, "Well, well, well, I'm certainly amongst good friends. Hello Bluey, we've spent many times in the morgue together, when you were in the Traffic Accident Squad, eh?" They both shook hands strongly.

Bluey grinned, "Great to have you on board, mate."

Fred turned to Angela, "Lovely to be working with you again, Angel. I guess Steve has approved of you working in the same building?"

Angela nodded, "He's just thrilled that I'm working with Jane, Doc, and I'm chuffed that you are joining us. What a fantastic team! Hope we get our first case soon, Boss." She looked over to Jane.

Jane nodded. "It's time for coffee. While Fred and I eat our late lunch, I'll start to tell you about our first case."

Ho sat, hands folded on his desk, staring straight into the face of Pierre de Jong. "When did you last see your father, Pierre?"

"Yesterday morning, Sir. He called in at my flat very early. Woke me up as a matter of fact, as it was only 7 am."

"That's not very early for a working lad like you. What do you do exactly?"

"I work from home. I'm a student and I also do IT part-time. I visit homes and help people with their computers and such." His hands were trembling and he started to sniff. "It's been a shock. I can't think straight...I...I..."

Charlie Chan leaned forward, "Would you like a drink of water, or some coffee perhaps?"

Pierre took a deep breath and swallowed, and his Adam's apple bobbed up and down. "Some water would be OK."

Chan got up and poured some water into a plastic cup from the nearby water cooler and brought it back to the table. "There you go, mate."

Steve liked it when Charlie played the Jeckle and Hyde policeman in interviews. They had planned it this way before talking with Pierre. Ho was not happy with the way Pierre had taken the death of his father so calmly, but at the same time had been quite nervous and agitated, and constantly sniffing like someone addicted to drugs.

Ho asked, "We haven't cautioned you or anything. We just need to clear up a few facts, that's all."

Charlie raised his voice, "Who was the woman in your flat, Pierre? Girlfriend? Lover? A pro?"

Pierre slammed his fist on the table. "Don't you call Loretta a prostitute. She's a good friend, she's a senior theatre nurse at Melbourne Central Hospital. She didn't want to drive home last night because she had one drink too many, and she was tired...and...and..."

Chan shook his head. "Cut the baloney, Pierre. She's your girlfriend. Loretta who?"

"Loretta Stevens." Pierre seemed to visibly shrink into the chair. He started sniffing again.

"Do you sniff cocaine?" asked Chan.

"Occasionally. So what!" was the reply as Pierre pouted. "Are you going to charge me for possession or something?"

"That's all for now, Pierre. We'll probably need to chat to you again. I'm sorry about your father's death. It's not easy doing an ID like you just did," said Ho. "You can go now."

"Thanks for nothing. I hated him!" With that last remark, the victim's son stormed out of the office.

Steve Ho looked at Charlie Chan then slapped him on the back. "Well done, mate. You got him to say that he hated his father. But that's not enough to charge him with anything at the moment. We won't be able to do much more today. We'll have to wait for the autopsy to be finished. Mary won't be back until later with her report from the autopsy anyway."

"Want me to try and set up an interview with the lovely Loretta Stevens tomorrow morning, Boss?"

"Good idea. She'll hopefully give us more insight into Pierre. Can't see what a senior nurse sees in such a plonker...unless it's simply a sexual thing!" Steve Ho grinned at Charlie Chan. "Well, it's time for me to go and pick up the twins from Angel's Mum & Dad's place, take them home and keep them amused until Angel gets home."

"Okay, Boss. See you first thing tomorrow," replied Chan.

Jane sat at the long conference table with her team. She handed out photocopies of the report that she had received from the Assistant

Commissioner before she had gone to see Doctor Fred Harvey to offer him the new job.

"Sorry about pretending that we didn't have a case yet, but I wanted to get Fred here first."

"We're all ears, Jane, go ahead!" said Fred.

"Victorian MP John Polites, and his wife Janet asked the coroner if he could have his daughter Vicki's body exhumed and re-autopsied. They found it hard to believe the first Coroner's report that their six-year-old daughter fell accidentally downstairs and killed herself."

"When did she die, Boss?" asked Angela Nguyen.

"Four weeks ago, today. The Coroner agreed to the request, and yesterday a second autopsy was done by a different pathologist. The findings show that she had bruising on her arms and throat, hardly an accident it seems. The bruising didn't show up in the first autopsy, which was done the day she died. The parents wanted a quick funeral after her organs had been donated. I know she died recently, but it was decided to pass over this case to us as a cold case."

Angela remarked, "How unusual!"

"Yes, it is, but Homicide have their hands full, and so we got our first 'technically cold' case." Replied Jane.

"So what is our first step, Boss?" asked Angela.

"Firstly, for Fred here to check the reports and perhaps the body again before she is re-buried the day after tomorrow. That's the most urgent thing. In the meantime, Bluey and Angel, you two can start checking all the details again on the first inquiry...such as what happened on the night she died, and recheck the times of the parents' alibis. They were apparently at a Government dinner. We also need to check what the hell the babysitter was doing when Vicki died. Oh, and our MP has finally admitted that he had previous threats to his family. This can be done more slowly and carefully, we don't want to leave any stone unturned."

Angela got up and looked at her watch, "I'll read these papers first, Boss, and then Bluey and I can sort out which witnesses to talk to tomorrow."

"Yep, good idea, Angel. Let's go through the paperwork together. Two heads will be better than one, and it will be better to proceed carefully in this Squad...right, Boss?"

"Absolutely! Well done, you two. A good first day on the job. At least you don't have to work through the night like your old job, eh?"

Fred got up and stretched. "Jane, I'm going to go and view the body now...it'll be better sooner, and I want to see the bruising for myself. Then I can compare with the report as I go. Not often that a second autopsy is done on a body missing organs from the first one because of organ donations. The parents have to be commended for that magnanimous decision at that awful time. I wonder how many lives she saved. I'll see you all tomorrow morning, folks!" With those words, Fred Harvey was gone.

Jane watched Angela and Stan going through the reports on the table, making notes and marking things on the whiteboard ready for the morning conference. She went to her office and started to sift through all the papers that required her signature first, then slowly went through Vicki Polites' case file.

Yes, Fred, what wonderful people they were during that traumatic time, to even contemplate giving authority for their precious daughter's organs to be donated. It was so lucky that the babysitter was a nurse, and was giving CPR to keep her breathing until the ambulance arrived. She snapped herself out of her thoughts as she heard Angela and Stan starting to pack up ready to go home.

"'Nite, Boss, see you in the morning," called out Angela.

"Time for you to go home, Boss," said Stan as he peered at her around the door.

He was right. She packed up quickly and left, locking the door behind her.

Yes it's good to be back at the pointy end!

It was over an hour later before Jane finally drove up the long driveway at *Wyndales*. The front door opened and Sassy and Spunky whizzed outside to greet her. Oliver stood at the door, a glass of red wine in hand. "Welcome home, my love. I like this new job of yours...you're home at a decent hour!"

They sat down on the back verandah, sipped on the wine, and nibbled some cheese and biscuits.

"Had a good day?" asked Jane.

"Yes, I did. And obviously you did too. Tell me about your day first, and then I'll tell you about my day, involving a girl having nightmares about being killed."

Later, whilst eating their dinner, Jane started to tell Oliver about Vicki Polites' organ donations given to needy recipients whilst she was kept artificially alive. Oliver's eyes opened wide. "Jane, I'll pour another glass for us both. I think you will be more than interested in my case...if I'm right about certain dates."

"Dates? What dates in particular? Why is your case more than interesting?" Jane felt a surge of excitement run through her veins like an electric shock. "Are these cases connected?"

Oliver grabbed a notepad, and showed her his notes and read them aloud to her. "Your victim, Vicki Polites, died four weeks ago today, and was taken to Melbourne Central Hospital. My case study, was called into Melbourne

Central Hospital four weeks ago today urgently, where she was given a compatible heart from an accident victim!"

Jane gasped, and took a large sip of wine. "Oh my God! This is almost spooky."

"Jane, you haven't experienced any of the supernatural stuff since our Amy died in birth five years ago."

"I'm not sure, Oliver, but combined with the look on your face and those same dates...it's too much of a coincidence, isn't it?"

She grabbed her mobile. "I'll see if Fred has finished viewing our victim. By the way, he's my squad's forensic adviser."

"I guessed that, my love."

"Fred? Have you finished looking at Vicki's body? Yep...uhuh..." she paced back and forth as she talked, and Oliver watched in amusement. "So it's definitely murder then? Go home, Fred. You need your beauty sleep, mate. See you in the morning. Bye."

"So? Tell me more about your victim while I pour some coffee, my love."

"Well obviously Fred couldn't view everything because of the donations. The main thing that is now showing on her body are bruise marks on her throat, and arms. It looks like she was forcibly pushed down the stairs and didn't accidentally fall as was the first coroner's finding."

"The thing I find most interesting, is the fact that your victim, Vicki, and my client, were both in the Melbourne Central Hospital on the same day...AND my Jenny was the recipient of a young person's heart the same day. Apparently, the donor died as a result of an accident. I wonder what type of accident was noted in the official hospital files."

"Absolutely, I have a strange feeling that your Jenny's nightmares might be her recipient's soul or ghost or whatever communicating through her new heart, trying to tell everyone that her previous owner's death wasn't an accident!"

"Current research has found that some organ donor recipients...especially those who received hearts seem to inherit some of the traits of their donor!"

"Oliver, is this knowledge part of your research into patients near death experiences?"

"Sort of... but there's another branch of the research, which I haven't really gone into in depth, yet."

Jane said, "The supernatural?"

Oliver replied, "Steady on Jane, don't let your imagination run away, we have both decided a few years ago that your supernatural insights and communication with the dead have faded, and may even have disappeared for good after your brain injuries finally healed...

Jane sat down and sighed. "I really think our cases are linked, Oliver. Maybe..."

"Maybe what?"

"If your client got Vicki's heart ...maybe that's where her dreams are coming from."

"Hey now, Jane," Oliver reassured her, "Don't let your imagination run away with you. It's been so long..."

"I know. It's just, it's a feeling I have. But you know, regardless of whether that's what it is, I have a perfect name for this case file!"

"What's that?"

"Haunted Heart." Jane smiled.

Day Two

At nine o'clock the next morning, Jane Doe, Stan Johnson, and Angela Nguyen were seated around the conference table in the Special Cold Case office, sipping from their mugs of coffee, listening to Doctor Fred Harvey.

Fred's deep brown eyes scanned his attentive audience, who each had their iPads open, ready to take notes. He tapped his own and the first image appeared on the interactive whiteboard behind him. He stroked his grey beard, pursed his lips, and then started talking.

"As you can see, this is a picture I took of Vicki's body...in fact the first time I saw her in the morgue." He paused briefly, peering over his reading glasses and pointed at Vicki's face. "The first thing I noticed were the bruise marks around her throat, then..." He put up another photo and pointed at several places on her upper arms, "more bruising here and here. These bruises were not mentioned in the first autopsy and certainly didn't show in the original photos taken by police, before the transplant organs were retrieved from her body at the Melbourne Central Hospital."

Harvey then showed the earlier photos adjacent to the recent ones. "You can see the differences."

Angela raised her hand, "Doc, why didn't the bruising show up at the hospital?"

Fred Harvey smiled, "Good question, Angel. It's simply because the bruising wasn't at the skin surface at that time. Bruising often comes to the surface a day or two later. You know what it's like...you suddenly see a bruise on your knee, and wonder *when did that happen*? And you remember that you'd knocked your knee against the table leg a couple of days earlier."

"Her parents had a quick funeral after the operation, didn't they?" remarked Stan. "That's why no one noticed the bruises!"

"Got it in one, Bluey."

Stan sipped from his mug, "Yeah, we found that quite often after motor accidents, when I worked in the traffic squad, that if the autopsy was delayed because of a backlog at the morgue, the bruising was much deeper a day or two later...oh crap, I've just spilled some coffee down my new tie. I'll be straight back." Stan stomped out to the kitchenette. Everyone giggled as the tap was turned on in the next room as they heard him mutter, "Shit! My missus will kill me. This was my anniversary present that she gave me a month before she died!" A minute later, he returned and eased his big frame onto the chair. He straightened his slightly wet tie, and ran his hand through his ginger hair.

Jane cleared her throat, "Bluey, for heaven's sake take the bloody tie off! It's not formal in here. And besides, you look uncomfortable with it on."

Stan gave a big sigh "Thanks Boss, I hate wearing ties anyway. They always remind me of funerals and weddings...not necessarily in that order, mind you."

Laughter echoed around the table.

Fred turned off the photo show and sat down at the table with the rest of the squad.

"It's the bruising that's inconsistent with an accident. As you could see, the bruises have left the pattern of fingers on her upper arms and throat. My findings are pretty obvious. Vicki Polites didn't simply fall down the stairs in her home...she was dragged along and pushed. It was murder."

"Doc, why didn't her parents notice anything at the funeral parlour the next day after the transplant organs were taken?" asked Jane.

"Quite simple, my dear. The funeral parlour had her dressed up in a long-sleeved frock, which had a high neckline. So everything was nicely covered up," he responded. "That's all I can say, really. So now it's up to you experts to find her murderer!"

Jane was the first to get up. "Thanks, Fred. We may need you later on in this case to practise your magic and do some testing of DNA samples and fingerprints."

"It will be my pleasure, ma'am!" Fred bowed his head towards Jane. "Well, I'm off to do some paperwork to finalise my official transfer to this squad. I'll catch up with you all later." He grabbed his iPad, put it into his satchel, and went to the door. "Bye folks."

"I can't help but love that guy," said Angela.

"Careful Angel, Steve will get jealous," quipped Stan.

"Nah, not the same kind of love...Fred is more like an old cuddly teddy bear I used to have as a kid."

Jane grinned. "Now, you two need to do some paperwork too. I'm off to see Vicki's parents at their home. I have an appointment at 11 am. So I'd better leave now. I'll call you before I leave there with any information I might get."

With those words, Jane left the office.

Jane pulled up her car outside the Polites' house, situated in the leafy suburb of Glen Iris. *What a lovely house! Looks like double clinker brick, similar to my parents.* Jane picked up her satchel which contained her iPad and digital recorder. She'd need those. *Hmm, genuine wrought iron gate...gosh this brings back memories!*

She went to the front door and pressed the bell button. A few moments later, the door was opened by the familiar face of MP John Polites. His face was often on television and in the papers.

"Come in, we were expecting you. Nice to meet you in person, Detective Chief Superintendent Doe."

"Please call me Jane, my title is a mouthful at the best of times," she responded. She followed him down the entrance passage and turned left into the main lounge room. By habit, she took in his appearance. *Tallish, olive skin, black hair. Typical Greek heritage.*

Janet Polites rose from the couch as Jane entered. She put out her hand in greeting.

"Nice to meet you, Ma'am." She ushered Jane to a big leather chair near the coffee table, where the aroma of freshly brewed coffee wafted into Jane's nostrils.

"Thanks, Janet. Please, just call me Jane." She smiled.

Janet sighed, and then smiled back at Jane. "Sure." She flicked her long blond hair back from her pale face, "Would you like milk with your coffee, Jane?"

"Yes, that will be perfect."

Five minutes later, after general pleasantries about the cold weather and what a lovely house and garden the Polites had, Jane turned the topic to the reason for her visit.

"This morning, we got the results of the second autopsy on Vicki."

Janet gasped, and covered her mouth with her hand. "It's different to the first one, isn't it, or you wouldn't be here!"

Jane was sitting next to Janet on the couch. She immediately put her hand on Janet's arm, and replied softly, "Yes, we now have additional information about her death."

John Polites took a deep breath and his dark brown eyes looked straight into Jane's as he spoke. "She was murdered, wasn't she?"

"Yes, I'm afraid there's definite evidence proving this now," Jane nodded. "When she was first examined by the doctors at the hospital, and then at the morgue after the transplanted organs had been retrieved for suitable recipients, there were some bruises not showing. Because she was dressed later at the funeral parlour in her favourite long sleeved dress with a high collar, some first signs of bruising were not seen. It takes a day or so before deep bruising comes to the surface..." She paused briefly. "Sorry about the detail, but I think it's best you know the facts..."

To her surprise, it was Janet who was the first to talk.

"Thanks, Jane. We wanted the truth; that's why we asked the Coroner to do a second autopsy. It was so unlike Vicki to walk around in the dark, or fall downstairs. She was a good little athlete, and liked going to the local gym. In fact, the instructors said she had remarkable balance and reflexes."

John then added, "We had received those threats, as you know. So we could only think that someone possibly wanted to harm her or to get at us in some warped way...what a bastard! I'd better not get near whoever killed Vicki..." He stopped, his voice cracking with emotion.

"It's now my squad's job to find her murderer so you can move on, and Vicki can be finally laid to rest in peace. If you can think of anything, please give me a call at any time." She passed a business card across to each of them. "Would it be possible for me to see Vicki's bedroom and the staircase?"

"Of course! We'll show you...anything to help," said John, and they all got up. Jane followed them out to the foot of the staircase, which was opposite the lounge room door, on the right side of the entrance hall. The stairs were steep, with a landing at the top that led to a large room to the right and a closed door on the left. Janet was first to the unopened door. She took a deep breath, turned the knob, and then beckoned Jane through. "This is...*was*...Vicki's room. It's exactly the same as the day she died... I... I couldn't bear to change anything."

"I understand, don't worry. In fact, this is a bonus for us I'll get our forensic people to come and check everything. Hopefully we'll find something to help us. By the way, do you mind if I take some photos?"

"That's not a problem. As we said, we'll do anything to help you," responded Janet. "We'll leave you to check and look at Vicki's room. Just call us if you need something."

With that last comment, Janet and John went downstairs, leaving Jane alone in Vicki's room.

Heck, it's a perfect time capsule for evidence! There's dust on the desk too, so this hasn't been cleaned since her death. I'll call Angel and Bluey to bring Forensic people out here to check for finger prints and take DNA samples from Vicki's parents and the babysitter, Loretta, if she is available...come to think of it, we need to interview this Loretta! She phoned her office, and Angela Nguyen answered after the first ring.

"Boss? How's it going out there?"

Jane filled her in on her chat with the Polites. "This room is going to be great for collecting evidence, as it hasn't been opened or cleaned since the day Vicki died."

"Crikey, a mausoleum? Hope we can solve this one, Boss, so these poor people can get on with life."

"My feelings too... Oh, could you also arrange to get an interview with the babysitter, Loretta? We can get a DNA sample and fingerprints from her at that time. I'll see you soon."

Jane looked around the room. *Typical seven-year-old, complete with school books on her desk by the window. Ah, obviously a favourite teddy, sitting there on the bed...nice shaggy teddy too, not unlike my old teddy at home in our bedroom.*

Above the bed was an old oil painting of a happy clown holding a Labrador puppy.

This painting's crooked. It's been moved, must check for fingerprints and DNA. Maybe the murderer touched this.

Jane put on her rubber gloves, pulled out her iPad and took some photos of the room, including the desk, painting, the bed and the teddy. She spent a good half hour exploring the whole room, including the books in the bookcase. She found Vicki's diary in her bedside table. To her dismay, it contained very little except for the mundane comments of someone her age about school, the weather, going to Gym, and wanting a puppy like the one in the painting for her next birthday. She slipped her iPad back into her satchel then leaned across the bed and picked up the teddy. She walked over to the window.

"Hello teddy, what's your name, I wonder. Bet you're missing Vicki, old fellow. Her mum and dad are too. I promise I'll find who killed her..." Jane felt a cold draft, which sent a shiver of excitement through her body. She turned around and gasped. The ghostly image of Vicki Polites was sitting on the bed, smiling at her.

Hell, I can see ghosts again! Don't frighten her, Jane. "Hello Vicki..."

The door of the bedroom opened, the ghost's imaged immediately disappeared. It was Janet, standing in the doorway. "Sorry to disturb you, but there are some police at the door asking for you."

Damn it! Jane put the teddy back on the bed.

"Thanks Janet, that'll be my squad. I've asked them to come and get official fingerprints from this room, plus DNA samples. We'll also need such samples from yourself and your husband, simply to separate evidence gathered that doesn't match yours or Vicki's."

"You think you'll find the murderer's prints?"

"Time will tell. This could be a slow process. The good thing is that this room hasn't really been disturbed much since Vicki died. By the way, this painting is an antique, isn't it?"

"Yes, Vicki was with John and me when we were looking through some antique shops at High Street, in Malvern. She took one look at this painting and wanted it for her birthday. We only paid fifty dollars for it. It's been valued at over four thousand! That was a bit over a year ago... Of course, we knew that she also wanted a puppy like that one for her next birthday...which is in two weeks' time." Janet's lip quivered. Jane put her hand on Janet's shoulder.

"Come on, let's go down and I'll introduce my team to you."

Angela and Stan had already introduced themselves to John Polites. Jane's eyes widened when she saw Doctor Fred Harvey standing there, complete with his forensic kit at the ready.

"I came to collect the DNA and help with the fingerprinting. Vicki's fingerprints and DNA are on file already." He explained, seeing her surprise, "I'll take everything back to the office to process this afternoon. We should have some results by tomorrow. I already have Mr Polites' DNA and fingerprints." He turned towards Janet. "May I get yours now, Mrs Polites?" said Fred.

"Certainly, Doctor," replied Janet.

Stan beckoned Jane over and quietly spoke to her.

"The babysitter is currently interstate, Boss, and should be back in Melbourne sometime tomorrow. We can contact her then," said Stan.

Jane nodded. "Good." She turned to Angela and said, "Let's get to work upstairs. Doc, you can follow up when you're ready."

The team got fingerprints and DNA samples of the painting, the desk, the teddy on the bed and around the door. Fred nodded at the Polites, who were watching him work.

"Might look like over-kill, pardon the expression, but sometimes the murderer thinks about the door knob, but forgets that they also actually touched the door or door frame."

The team finally left the Polites' house an hour later, after Jane collected copies of recent photos of Vicki that she got from her parents. They returned to the office, grabbed sandwiches and pies to eat, then finally sat down at the conference table to discuss their updates over coffee. Within five minutes, Fred joined them from his mini-laboratory room.

"Well folks, we have fingerprints of Vicki's mum and dad, and of course Vicki. There are two sets of different prints that are unaccounted for. Hopefully one set will belong to Loretta Stevens..."

"The other set were found on the teddy's leather pads, and on the painting frame."

"The murderer's?" exclaimed Jane.

"Fingers crossed that they will match a future prime suspect, Jane," Fred smiled.

Whilst Jane and her team were at the Polites' home, Steve Ho and his Special Crime Squad had been interviewing associates of Professor Johann de Jong, their murder victim.

Their interviews with other surgeons at the Melbourne Central hospital and several theatre nurses yielded a lack of information.

Finally, Sister Susan Grant gave some valuable information.

Ho asked, "I've been told that Doctor Stapleton, the senior pathologist at the morgue, has left the hospital. Do you know where he went?"

Susan replied, "Yes, I do. He now owns and runs a funeral parlour in St. Kilda. A fellow theatre nurse that I work with at the hospital is rumoured to do some *moonlighting* when off shift at the morgue, with Stapleton. I think this is a bit weird, personally. Just thought you'd like to know about these rumours."

Ho replied, "This is just the sort of information we need. Thanks, Susan. Is there anything else that you want to tell us?"

Susan blushed, and then said, "Well it's rather personal, but I must tell you. It could help you find Johann's murderer... I always admired his work, and liked working in theatre with him. We became very close...I also agreed with his campaign about the possibilities of *bad* organs and tissues in this country either illegally imported or locally obtained. The latter was a huge worry of his. We often worried about the paperwork...whether it was falsified. I think Johann was getting too close to something illegal in the hospital. There were rumours about lights on in the hospital morgue after hours. Is this the sort of information you need?"

Ho responded. "Exactly! Susan, just said that you and the Professor became very close..."

Susan smiled. "We became lovers...I'm worried about my safety. Johann took me out to dinner, a few times...no, quite a lot really...maybe someone knew about our relationship and also knew that Johann was close to finding out about the illegal use of the morgue?"

Mary Lamb smiled at Susan and said, "You were in love with him?"

Susan sighed, and shrugged her shoulders. "His wife died a few years ago during childbirth. The daughter was stillborn. It was so sad. His son Pierre, well, he's a bit of a useless fellow...what I'd call a professional student who doesn't really want to work for a living. He didn't get on with his father. I don't know why, because Johann did everything for Pierre... perhaps too much. I now think that he actually blamed his mother's death in childbirth on his father, for getting her pregnant at an older age..."

After Susan's interview, Steve Ho had a quick conference with his team.

"This might be just what we need."

"Boss, the differences between father and son match up with Pierre's interview. Spoilt brat! I for one would put him in as a possible suspect along with his bit of fluff, Loretta Stevens. What do you think?" asked Chan.

"Agreed... We'll put them on the suspect list for now. We'll add others as they're interviewed."

There was a knock at Ho's door. "Come in!"

"It's Sergeant Standing. We've just received copies of the autopsy report on de Jong. I guess you have the originals?"

"Hello Jason, take a seat. Mary, Charlie and I were just about to talk about the results. Thanks for coming in."

They listened intently as Ho read the report.

"Professor Johann de Jong didn't drown, as we guessed, as there was no water in his lungs. He was dead when he was put into the lake. Stomach contents have shown a small amount of alcohol but more importantly, traces of chloral hydrate, quote: a drug originally discovered through chlorination or halogenation of ethanol in 1832 by Justus von Liebig in Gieben. Sedative properties, because of its easy synthesis were used recreationally in the late 19th Century. Chloral hydrate is soluble in both water and alcohol readily forming concentrated solutions. A solution of chloral hydrate in alcohol called *knockout* drops was used to prepare a Micky Finn."

"My, this new senior pathologist likes his history, doesn't he? But it certainly explains why de Jong hadn't defended himself," remarked Standing.

Ho laughed, and continued, "You're right there, Jason. Okay, the report continues: 'The victim was drugged. Blood samples showed large doses of Sodium thiopental... commonly used as an ultra-short barbiturate in inductions phase of general anaesthesia. This drug rapidly reaches the brain and causes unconsciousness. The drug is used intravenously for euthanasia in Belgium and the Netherlands, where allowed by law. It's also used in thirty-four states in the U.S.A to execute prisoner by lethal injection.'" Ho looked up from the document briefly, seeing the rapt faces of his audience, and then continued, "'So we can assume rightly that de Jong was given chloral hydrate in a glass of alcohol, which also assumes that he trusted or knew the killers. When he was immobilised, he was given the lethal dose of sodium thiopental to stop his breathing and heart...thus causing death. His body was then taken to the lake late at night, when no one was around. His body was found the next morning by the family walking their dog.'"

Ho stretched in his chair, "We now have the cause of death, and the most obvious motive being the victim's recent public comments regarding the possible illegal imports or local illegal collection of body parts and organs. Okay, I want everyone to go through all their notes again and double check the alibis of Doctor Aaron Brown, supervisor of the Melbourne

Central Hospital morgue, and Doctor Henry Stapleton, formerly of the Melbourne Central Morgue who now owns and runs a funeral parlour in St. Kilda. Also check our Loretta Stevens' shift roster and movements at the time of de Jong's death. Find out how long she's been interstate. And finally, Pierre de Jong's movements also need to be double checked."

The meeting had finished, and Sergeant Jason Standing returned to his office in Broadmeadows to get his team to help check alibis.

Ho then went down to the cafe on the ground floor to take a short break. To his delight, Jane was also arriving at the café for a break.

"Hello, Jane... can we talk?"

Steve and Jane shared their day's activities and suspects as they sipped coffee. Jane's eyes widened when Ho talked about one suspect they needed to interview, Loretta Stevens, who was in Sydney and should be returning the next day.

"Loretta Stevens! She's one who we need to interview too. She was the babysitter of my cold case victim, Vicki Polites, at the time of her death."

"Now that's really interesting, Jane, as she's supposedly Pierre de Jong's girlfriend. She was with him early...very early...in the morning when the Broadmeadow's CID called to inform him of his father's death."

"Pierre's father was the surgeon who transplanted the new heart into my victim, Steve! Our cases are connected, I'm sure of it."

"I agree with you, Jane. It's interesting that your Vicki Polites' parents agreed to donate her organs to those in need of transplants on the day she died at the Melbourne Central Hospital."

"Okay, let's co-ordinate information we receive from our interviews with Loretta, which will hopefully be sometime tomorrow. What do you say?"

"Agreed. This is one way to find out if our cases really are connected. I'll catch up with you after our separate interviews. As I said before, it's nice to work or should I say co-ordinate with you again."

The two friends then left the cafe and returned to their offices.

Jane spent another hour clearing up the mandatory paperwork and after a brief chat with her team, told them to go home and be fresh for the next day.

She drove home, listening to some light classical music whilst she thought about her brief ghostly sighting that morning.

I can see ghosts again! I must try and communicate verbally with Vicki next time. Yes there must be a next time.

As Jane opened the front door at *Wyndales,* Spunky and Sassy rushed to greet her. The food in the crock pot that Oliver had set up after she left in the morning smelled delicious!

"God, I'm lucky I married you, Oliver."

"What you're really saying is 'thank God you can cook, Oliver.'" He grinned, "But it's my pleasure, my love. I have more time than you, as my office is only a short drive away, so I could set up the crock pot to cook slowly ready for when we both got home...and voila! Let's relax first, with a glass of wine."

"Great idea, hang on while I change into my warm tracksuit and *Ugg* boots."

After dinner, they returned to the lounge and the fire to drink coffee and indulge in a cheese platter with biscuits.

"You first, my dear. You've been busting to tell me something all through dinner, even though I wanted you to relax first for a change. So how was your day?"

Jane pushed a lock of her auburn hair away from her face. "I saw Vicki's ghost today!" she blurted.

Oliver gasped. "Where was she? Did she talk to you? Were you alone?"

"Slow down," Jane laughed, "Yes I was alone, she was sitting on her bed. And no, she didn't talk to me, mainly because her mother came into her bedroom and interrupted our meeting, damn it! But she was definitely there. I was talking to her teddy that I'd picked up off the bed, asking him if he missed her, and I felt a cold draft behind me...and there she was! Spooky, but on the other hand, I was thrilled to be able to see the ghost of a victim again!"

"I guess you'll try to see her again, and hopefully communicate with her?"

"Of course. But it would have to be on her terms somehow... I'll think of a way. The room had been virtually closed for the past month since her death."

"Wow, a time-capsule. What a bonus for forensics, my love. Did they find anything?"

"Well, there were fingerprints of her parents, and of course Vicki, plus two separate sets of prints. One set mainly around the door, the other on the frame of the painting...which we hope at least one set will belong to her killer. The painting was crooked on the wall, and hadn't been straightened, so I reckon Vicki's intruder had moved it. We also have DNA samples which will be cross-matched with Vicki's parents, and of course her babysitter, Loretta...when she returns from Sydney tomorrow...plus the other mystery person's DNA which was collected from the teddy and picture frame." Jane paused, then added, "And how was your day, Oliver?"

"Fascinating! My client mentioned in her dream that the intruder talked in a hoarse whisper and that she wasn't sure if it was a male or female.

Whenever she tried to sit up or get out of the bed, this person immediately pushed her down. He teased her with her teddy bear."

"Teddy bear?" gasped Jane. "Sorry, go on."

"Eventually she remembered flashes of trying to push past this person, who grabbed her by her arms. She thinks she kicked out and connected with his shins...note she said *his,* I checked on that later. She said it was strong enough to be a man."

"Fred showed us the second autopsy results today...we saw the comparisons between the original photos and the new ones which definitely showed deep bruise marks, indicating strong fingers on her upper arms...so your client's dream is correct. Plus, there were bruise marks on her throat."

"So, as we discussed last night, she was held, still struggling, then pushed down the stairs," Oliver mused, "Her tale of her nightmare matches what the autopsy revealed today. God, put that together with your Vicki trying to contact you...it could to be Vicki's heart contacting the real world through her dreams, just like you said! Hell!"

Jane nodded. "Perhaps Vicki had been drugged before she went to sleep, because she keeps telling you that she felt so sleepy that night. Has she described the house or room to you?"

"Yes, she remembered a lot more today. She told me that she was in a two storied house. Her bedroom was upstairs, which is weird, because her mother told me after our consultation that she has never slept in a two storied house in her life! She also talked about a puppy and a teddy called Harry and a clown..."

"Wait a moment!" Jane picked up her tablet opened it and handed it over to Oliver, her eyes wide. "Take a peek at these pictures. They will make your skin crawl."

Oliver looked through the photos that Jane had taken at the Polites' house that morning. "Well, well, well...there's Harry, the teddy, and the Labrador puppy is being held by a clown in the painting above the bed." He looked straight at Jane, a big grin across his face. "This proves that it's your Vicki's ghost or soul or whatever haunting my client, through Vicki's transplanted heart. Vicki is literally telling us through her, how she died! Jane, there's evidence in medical journals that a donor's organ, particularly a heart, can insert feelings or thoughts on its new host body. I read transcripts about donor recipient's knowing things that they have never experienced, which have proven to be things that the donor, in the case of siblings or parents has actually done."

"Oliver, I need to prove this via normal police procedure, just like the cases of my former victims. But I must admit, if we are right, I can only hope our ghost will contact me again."

Oliver shuffled through pages on his desk. A photo dropped onto the floor and Jane retrieved it. "Thanks Jane, Jenny's pretty, isn't she? Hell, I mentioned her name."

"Yes, she's pretty... Oh God, Oliver, that's my ghost!"

"Jane, can I take a copy of the teddy and the clown and puppy painting to show to her tomorrow? I think we'll get a definite positive reaction."

"Good idea, but please don't tell her where you got them from. I'm convinced that the time of death plus the transplant of Vicki's heart in the same hospital the next day is an obvious fact." Jane got up and stood in front of the fire. Her hazel eyes sparkled in the light of the flames. "Let's face it, I find it hard to believe that the Melbourne Central did two heart transplants on the same day, especially given the fact that Professor de Jong is the transplant specialist. I couldn't imagine him doing two such operations in the same day."

Oliver put his empty coffee mug on the tray. "I'll use my medical contacts at the Melbourne Central Hospital to see if I can get the record of the donor's name."

"I'm looking forward to interviewing Vicki's babysitter tomorrow." Jane yawned. "Look at the time...I think I need my beauty sleep." Oliver put the fire screen in place, and they went to bed.

Day Three

At 11 am the next morning, Jane sat down next to Stan Johnson to interview Sister Loretta Stevens.

Jane looked Loretta straight into her brown eyes for a few moments before starting. *Dark brown hair, well groomed, average height, slender build... but has well developed muscles. Bet she does body building work at a gym.* She cleared her throat, and then, after starting the recorder, went through the preliminary cautions and advising her of her rights.

"Loretta, I believe you've been interstate. Was it a short holiday or business?"

Loretta pouted her bottom lip, "I have family in Sydney and I had some days in lieu owing to me, so I took them. So what's this got to do with me being here?"

Stan then asked, "You're a friend of the Polites?"

"I met them briefly a couple of years ago through two guys who suggested that I could babysit their daughter for them, that's all."

"What guys?"

She sighed. "I met them at a night club in King Street. That's all I know about them. Oh, they were proper gentlemen too; they both went to Melbourne Grammar together. Yes, I remember them saying that at the time. That's how they knew the Polites. They had friends whose kids went to the same school. One was called Peter or Pierre I think and the other was called Gray or Graham or whatever."

Time to change the direction. Lying bitch, she was Pierre's girlfriend, she must have known his surname!

"Tell us what happened on the night Vicki Polites died," she probed.

Loretta started to fidget in her chair and clasped her hands on the table in front of her tightly as she replied. "I went to their house early, as the Polites' had a special dinner at Government House that night. They were all dressed up to the nines. Janet was very glam in a silver long frock with a matching jacket, and John was in the usual penguin suit...you know the score." Her knuckles were turning white as she clutched her hands tighter. "The government car picked them up sharp at six. Vicki and I had some dinner that had been left for me to reheat in the microwave. I think they know I'm not much of a cook. Then we watched some TV. At about nine, I told Vicki it was time for bed."

Jane queried, "So nothing unusual happened whilst you were eating dinner, or while you watched TV?"

"Sheesh, I don't know. What do you mean?"

Stan prompted Loretta, "Such as a noise outside, a door opening, a noise in the kitchen...anything out of the normal noises that you were hearing watching the TV."

"Oh, earlier I heard a noise outside the back door. I went out to check, but saw nothing. It was probably a stray cat or something. I went back to the lounge and we continued to watch the programme."

"So after the show finished, you sent Vicki to bed, then what did you do?" asked Jane.

"I went upstairs to make sure Vicki was settled...she was. I'd actually added a mild sedative into her milk to help her sleep, as she was always a light sleeper, and had often come down stairs on previously occasions. I reckoned she needed some sleep. Bit of a highly strung kid, I thought."

"Did you have permission to give her this medication..." queried Jane.

Loretta's face turned pale, and Jane noticed a light sheen of perspiration on her forehead. *Good, now we've got you on the ropes, girl... we'll keep punching!* Jane continued her interrogation in a more forceful manner, leaning forward towards Loretta, who was sitting opposite, their faces almost touching.

"We'll need the exact medication that you gave her, and the dose, before you leave. You will, of course be answerable to the Polites for doing such a thing to their daughter without permission. Now did you continue to watch TV, or did you have a little tipple of wine from the Polites wine stock in the kitchen cupboard? Surely you can't tell me you didn't deserve it after a hard day in theatre before doing this extra job...money for jam, wasn't it?"

Loretta's face now started to flush a little, and she started to scowl at Jane.

"There was a bottle of red on the side kitchen bench that I'd noticed when I came back in after checking outside the back door. Okay, so I poured a glass from it. That's all I got, because it was then empty, so I put the empty bottle outside in the bin. I took the glass of wine back to the lounge room. It was about a quarter past ten by then, so I was looking forward to a quiet tipple before the Polites returned around eleven, as planned. I... I must have fallen asleep, 'cause the next thing I remember...I thought I was dreaming at first, but I wasn't...was Vicki screaming, then a heavy thump in the hallway. I got up slowly...I felt weird...and I went into the hall and I saw Vicki lying at the foot of the stairs. I phoned 000 and started CPR straight away, as she wasn't breathing at first. I got her breathing and kept her going until the paramedics arrived about ten minutes later. They took over and I was then able to phone her parents while the paras kept working on Vicki to stabilise her so she could be taken to Melbourne Central. We generally receive accident victims there in emergency, you know." Loretta finally slumped in her chair before continuing. "The Polites' arrived home just as the ambulance was about to leave for the hospital."

Stan leaned forward and said, "You heard Vicki scream first, before the thumping noise?"

"Hmm...yes. That's what woke me. I felt so sleepy, it was hard to get up at first. Then I heard the noise, the noise as she went down the stairs, obviously...then nothing..."

Stan asked her again, "Nothing? You didn't hear or see a door close or slam?"

"Hmm, let me think. I... I...oh yes, the front door wasn't shut properly...I didn't remember that before now..."

Stan continued his attack, "Loretta, did you shut the back door after you disposed of the wine bottle?"

Loretta was beginning to tremble slightly, as she replied, "I...I'm not sure. I'd had a couple of gulps out of the glass before I took the empty bottle outside. It went straight to my head, I...I don't remember if I did now. Why all these questions about the back door? You think Vicki didn't fall? What's going on?"

Jane looked at the now terrified Loretta and spoke quietly, "Vicki's parents asked the Coroner for a second autopsy. The results show that she was pushed down the stairs. There were bruises on her arms and around her mouth, suggesting that she'd been forced from her bedroom and then down the stairs."

Loretta's eyes bulged and her hands shook, "Oh My God! Someone killed her? Why didn't I hear anything?"

Jane replied, "Unfortunately it will be hard to prove that you could have possibly been drugged with that wine. The bottle was collected with other rubbish the next morning. Are you sure you didn't hear anything else?"

Loretta lowered her head and mumbled, "Maybe some footsteps, earlier, but I thought it was Vicki walking around. Then I dosed off again, then the scream and thumping on the stairs and... Hell, I'm not much of a witness, am I?"

Jane responded, "Loretta, I want you to take your time. Let's go through your story again...this time with the extra things that you can remember."

The interview finally finished thirty minutes later. Loretta was cautioned not to speak to anyone about the interview, and to be prepared to possibly come in again for further questioning, if required.

As Jane and Stan went to their desks, Angela immediately went up to Jane and said, "Detective Chief Inspector Ho would like to talk with you about their interview that they had with Loretta. Obviously, he wants to swap information."

Jane smiled at her, "Please do me a favour and inside this office, just refer to your husband as either Steve or Ho. I'd rather not have such formalities when it's only our squad in here." Her voice softened immediately, as Angela looked embarrassed. "It's okay, Angel, I'm not angry...actually I'm impressed that you wanted to say his full title, as you should if any *outsiders* were present in this office." She winked. "Besides we're personal friends, outside working hours!"

With that last remark, Jane picked up her mobile and rang Steve Ho. "Coffee's on, mate, come over and we can swap notes on Sister Loretta Stevens."

Steve arrived within five minutes, holding a file and a copy of his interview with Loretta.

"Okay Boss, tell me about your interview first, and I'll fill you in on ours. I think you'll be surprised at what we found out this morning about Sister Stevens."

"Steve, let's grab ourselves a cuppa and then we can go into the conference room so we won't disturb the others whilst they are catching up on paperwork here."

They also took two biscuits from the snack tin in the kitchenette.

"Nice set-up you've got here, Jane. I just wish they'd update our office sometime... when there's money available in the budget, of course!" He followed Jane into the conference room.

Jane then turned on the copy of her tape, and Steve Ho listened intently. When the tape finished, Jane looked at Steve and said, "I'll give you a copy of the transcript, seeing as our cases are overlapping with Loretta's involvement."

"Thanks Jane!" He stretched his arms above his head, "Wow, quite the lady this one! Now, I'll fill you in on what we found out from our side of the tracks." Ho opened his file. "I'll give you a copy of our transcript too. As you know, Loretta Stevens works in theatre at the Melbourne Central Hospital. She often worked with our murder victim, Professor Johann de Jong. In fact, she assisted de Jong when he transplanted a new heart into a young girl."

"What? When?"

"She was referring to an operation done a month ago..."

"Sorry, go on, I'm all ears..."

"The accident victim's heart was okayed for transfer to donate by her parents around midnight. The donor's body was kept on life support that night, so that the next day not only the heart, but the lungs, corneas and liver were taken out for possible transplant patients in waiting." He paused and took a long sip of coffee and a mouthful of biscuit, before continuing. "Hmm, I haven't had a teddy bear biscuit since this morning, when Angel, was packing Khan and Kylie's lunches." Steve grinned, sorry, I'm digressing. Loretta believes the lungs went to Sydney. The liver was apparently damaged by the fall down the stairs, and not right for transplant. The corneas were also taken out and sent to Adelaide. Loretta said that she had been involved counter witnessing the paperwork, as she had helped to convince the parents to donate their child's organs. The heart was matched very well with a Melbourne girl who was immediately brought in by her parents to be prepared for the operation the next day...."

"What was the date of the operation?"

Ho pointed to his file notes.

"Wow, very interesting! Do you know who the parents are?"

"Well... um... I shouldn't really tell you...but why are you asking?"

"Same day, same hospital, and one heart transplanted from my cold case victim, Vicki Polites, to another child? Plus the operation done by your murder victim, assisted by my victim's babysitter? Too many co-incidences here, mate!"

"Off the record, mind you...the heart was given to...no I shouldn't tell you..."

Jane touched his arm, "I know already. It was donated to a Jenny Summers."

"How did you know?"

"This is why I wanted to talk to you in private. Jenny is one of Oliver's patients. She has been having nightmares about being murdered in a two storied house and pushed downstairs. Which is exactly what happened to my cold case victim and that woman, Loretta, was present in the theatre during the transplant. Hell!"

"But she wouldn't have known the donor's name not even the surgeon would have known. That's what the etiquette is in transplants from cadavers."

"Yes, I know. I know the protocol. But let's face it, Loretta was present when Vicki's parents were consenting to their child's donation. She must have guessed where the donated heart came from. She's certainly quite a hard-nosed bitch; assisting in that operation when she actually knew the donor, and knew she was being taken to Melbourne Central Hospital!"

"You're not wrong there. Our cases appear to be more connected than we originally thought. I'm beginning to wonder about Loretta's involvement in the donation part. Did you know she was with her boyfriend the morning that he was told his father had been floating in Bridgewater Lake?"

"Pierre de Jong? Yes, Susan Grant gave up that info yesterday about Pierre's *bit of fluff,* Loretta. You could be right about the paperwork bit, too...let's face it, Pierre has a record for forgery. Could be more than a coincidence that Loretta was with Pierre that morning...but that's your case, mate."

Steven jotted some notes in his file, "Good point though, Jane! Apparently the excuse for her being at Pierre's place was that she was too tired to drive home...just a friend? Ha! And as soon as his father was murdered, Loretta went away for a few days to Sydney. So when we both started to try and contact her after Johann de Jong's body was found, she was unavailable! Convenient? Hmm, interesting facts though. It's also interesting that Loretta and the 'Pierre or Peter' she briefly mentioned in your interview as a casual night club friend has become a very, very close friend."

"Steve, I can only agree with what you've just said. It's so weird, the coincidences in each case too. Almost eerie..."

"Jane, I'm only asking this because of what Oliver's patient is dreaming...which is, to me, spooky stuff... After five years of not seeing anything supernatural, have you seen any ghosts since you've been back at the pointy end of work?"

"What? Um well, one reason why we're in this room alone is because of something I wanted to tell you earlier, as you know about my former paranormal powers. I briefly saw the ghost of my victim at the Polites' house, when I went to have an informal interview with them, and to see Vicki's room."

"Jane, that's fantastic! Did she speak to you, or communicate?"

"Her mother came into the room and she disappeared, but I'm hoping she'll try to contact me again when she feels confident. Oliver and I think that her soul, or ghost, or impression of her is still in her heart and is haunting Jenny Summers, giving her nightmares. She obviously wants the world to know that her death wasn't an accident. We know that for a fact now, anyway, but I'd dearly like to see her ghost again and hopefully communicate with her...I'll just have to be patient..."

Steve looked at Jane. "I won't tell a soul, Jane."

"Steve, does Angel know anything about my supernatural ability?"

"Well, I haven't said anything, but as you know, she's a highly intelligent person, and I think she put a few things together in her mind in our last case together five years ago. You know the file name only too well...*Severance Packages.* Angel suspected that you had some, well, let's call it *enlightened* information before you found the hard facts, especially with all the body parts being found after you changed areas. I simply told her it was pure luck...a policewoman's gut instinct...but yes I think she knows or at least suspects."

He got up, and gave her at brief hug.

"Are you okay? What does Oliver think about this latest meeting?"

"He's fascinated, as usual. It's one of his preoccupations after that wonderful academic paper he wrote about life and near death experiences recorded in hospitals. We really thought that my brain injuries were gradually and permanently healed over the last five years, which meant that these insights and sightings that I had back then, simply disappeared. But as soon as I got back into the pointy end of my job, dealing closely with violent death again...voila! My powers are back."

"Jane, I'm interviewing Pierre de Jong again tomorrow. I'll ask him the right questions without letting it slip that you know about his friendship with Loretta."

"Steve, could you also ask him about his so-called friend, Graham? If I could find out his name, maybe he could tell us more about Pierre's friendship with the Polites family."

"I'll get our transcript copy over to you straight away, so your team can read to it too. Our teams can start comparing notes. Nice to work with you again, Boss!" He winked. "Got to go now. Speak to you soon, Jane Doe." He turned and left the conference room, leaving Jane alone, her mind racing with the information that she had just received.

Jane quickly briefed her squad about what she and Steve Ho had been discussing, without any mention of ghosts.

"As you can see, our cases are now connected." She turned to Fred Harvey. "Fred, can you fill in the team on the procedures re Organ donations?"

Fred nodded, "Of course, my dear. Stating the obvious first; it's the hospital's duty to save life if at all possible. Organ donation is only considered after the patient is only being kept alive on life support. It is then that two independent senior doctors are asked to verify this. This was given, in Vicki's case, as she was only kept breathing and her heart pumping to keep her alive so organ donation was possible, after her parents' consent."

Angela then spoke, "So who decides which organs are donated to whom?"

"Good question, Angel. This is overseen by transplant physicians in each state, based on blood group, tissue type and on the waiting list, taking into account if they've been on dialysis for a long time. But finally, it is decided by a computer algorithm, when the donation is from a cadaver. This program is national, with only a few minor changes for each state. That's why Vicki's organs went to different states, packed in ice, cleaned, and sent by air urgently for their recipient. Obviously, the heart was a great match for Vicki's Melbourne recipient, who happened to be the same age."

Jane then gave her team a summary for their follow up work for the last hour of work.

"Okay, let's check up on what we've got on file to date, and what needs to be checked and recorded, such as the DNA tests."

"I'll have the DNA results you took ready by tomorrow," said Fred. "I'll see you all first thing in the morning."

Jane spent an hour at her desk, then told everyone to go home. She closed and locked the office door, and then headed to the lift and the car park. *It's going to be a long day tomorrow. But we're getting somewhere at last.*

As her usual habit, Jane drove north along the tree-lined St. Kilda Road, then through the city, now crowded with people, all seemingly in a hurry to go somewhere.

Shoppers, workers like me, all heading home after a day's work to their families...or maybe tourists, going to their hotels or perhaps a restaurant for a leisurely dinner, and then perhaps to one of the famous live theatres. Gosh it's been ages since Oliver and I went out to a show. Mind you, I'm happier simply going home to a wonderful welcome...and to relax!

Jane finally turned onto the Tullamarine Tollway, which eventually led to the Calder Highway and ultimately, the cosy little town of Gisborne, where their ten-hectare property, *Wyndales* was situated, on the southern side of the township.

An hour later, she was home. Oliver, Sassy, and Spunky greeted her in that order.

"My, what a lovely welcome as usual everyone...shall we all go out for a short walk before dinner? I feel like some fresh country air after being stuck in air-conditioning all day."

"Can't resist your offer, my love. I'll get the dogs' leads, and away we go..."

"Won't be a sec, Oliver. I need to change first."

Jane rushed into the bedroom and changed into her warm tracksuit, with wool socks and walking shoes, and then grabbed a thick jacket and woollen beanie. She went and joined the eager trio, who were waiting on the back verandah.

"Let's go!" said Oliver, and they walked down the back driveway that led to the paddocks where their herd of alpacas were grazing contentedly before they disappeared into the warmth of a shed at the back of the paddock.

"We do spoil them, don't we? They seem to love using the shed at night," remarked Jane.

"I can't blame them...it's going to drop to near freezing tonight, Jane. I've even put on Sassy and Spunky's winter coats."

Jane laughed, "I noticed. They're spoilt too."

The foursome walked up to the alpacas and patted some of them. The large gumtrees started to creak as the wind swirled. The faint smell of eucalyptus surrounded them.

"Hmm," Jane sighed, "I love that smell, Oliver." She shivered, "Our herd are lucky; they have their inbuilt thermal coats to keep them warm. What lovely thick wool they have!"

"Yes, they'll give us a great wool crop next spring, especially as a cold winter has been forecast. Brr! It's getting colder and darker...perhaps we'd better get back. By the way, have you seen Vicki's ghost again?"

"No, darn it. I think I'll have to wait for the right opportunity. I'd love to actually communicate with her though. Heck, you're not wrong; my teeth are starting to chatter with this cold wind... Hurry up!"

Jane jogged off in front of Oliver and the dogs. They finally caught up with her as she opened the back door, and they all rushed into the warm house.

"Hmm! I can smell that crock pot...chicken...yum. Shall I serve it up?" asked Jane as she shed her heavy coat.

"That sounds great. I'll get some wine to have with it. That walk in the cold evening air has made us all hungry." He opened a bottle, then turned around and looked at the two eager furry faces looking up at him. "But first, I'd better feed the dogs before they decide to chew my leg!"

He grinned at Jane who was lifting the lid of the crock pot, which had been slowly cooking their dinner all day. She took a deep breath.

"Yes, just perfect. Dinner will be served in exactly three minutes."

"I'll be right there, on time, with bottle in hand ready to pour."

Jane and Oliver spent the next hour, quietly enjoying their food, and discussing their work.

"Jenny certainly reacted positively to the photos that you took at the Polites house, Jane. She confirmed that the house in her dreams was exactly the same. She wanted to know where the house was...I told her that it belonged to friends...then she made an extraordinary remark."

"What did she say?"

"She said that she believed that the house belonged to the person whose heart was inside her. She was quite calm about it. She added that it was the only explanation, as she'd never actually been to that house, so how else could she have seen it so clearly in her dreams."

"Jenny's quite an astute young girl, isn't she? Did you confirm this to her?"

"I told her that it has been noted by other transplant patient recipients, like her, that sometimes organs...especially the heart...can implant their previous owner's feelings or experience on the recipient. But I also told her that I couldn't tell her who the house belonged to, because I hadn't taken the photos. I told her that one day, she might find more answers. She understood that she may never know the donor's name, but was obviously very grateful to the family for making such a brave decision at such a very *horrible* time for them. Yes, Jenny's a very mature young lady, hardly a girl anymore." He looked at Jane, then added, "What was your day like, my love?"

"We interviewed Loretta Stevens, Vicki Summer's babysitter who was with her on the night she was murdered. She was rather vague about what happened... I think, at first, she was trying to exaggerate the fact that she couldn't remember everything, but when pressed to relate everything that happened once again, we got the impression that she had genuinely been drugged with the wine that she'd found in the kitchen after they had eaten. Unfortunately, we can't prove that now, as the wine bottle was dumped in the next day's rubbish collection, and the glass had been washed the next morning in the dishwasher." Jane leaned forward in her chair and fiddled with her ponytail. "But later, I swapped notes with Steve Ho, who had also interviewed Loretta earlier in the morning. He said that Loretta had assisted Professor Johann de Jong in transplanting a new heart into Jenny on the same day as Vicki's heart was removed for transplant. I checked the hospital records later...there was only one heart transplant at Melbourne Central Hospital that day..."

"So not only are our cases are connected, but so is Steve's case... Wow! Sounds like Loretta is involved in some weird way with de Jong's murder...am I right?"

"Maybe. But we have to prove how and why, in both cases. But she's certainly a strong link between each case, and now a suspect to be checked out further. The casual friend she mentioned to me called 'Peter or Pierre' is actually Pierre de Jong, the professor's son and her current beau!"

"Crikey!"

"She was also present with Vicki's parents when they consented to the organ transplants, after it was confirmed that Vicki was officially only being kept alive by machinery. Steve and I were alone in the conference room when we swapped the interview details... He asked me if I'd seen any ghosts since I've been working at the *pointy end* again..."

"And you said yes?"

Jane nodded.

"Well, I'm pleased he asked. Between the three of us, your supernatural experiences have been kept secret, as they should be. But like Steve, I think that this special ability that you have can work so well in helping you to solve these types of cases." He took her hand and kissed it. "You're a very special lady, Detective Chief Superintendent Jane Doe, and I'm proud to be married to you." He leant over and gave her a light kiss.

"I'm just doing my job...but thanks!" grinned Jane and stretched her arms. "Oliver, I think we'd better clean up this table and get ready for bed. I'm feeling really tired all of a sudden."

"I can't blame you, my love. The past has come slap bang back to you the last few days, which will emotionally make you feel drained. I agree that it's time for your beauty sleep. I'll clean up. My first appointment isn't until ten tomorrow morning."

Jane got up and hugged him, and they kissed.

"Thank you for being you, Oliver. It's going to be a long day tomorrow."

She left the dining room and headed to the bedroom with a big smile on her face.

Day Four

Jane woke up earlier than usual. Her mind was full of all the combined information that matched with Ho's murder case and her cold case.

Heck I felt like a steam roller had rolled over me after dinner. I really need that sleep. I must try to surprise Oliver one night, and cook a nice dinner for him. Especially now I don't have to work such long and irregular hours anymore.

She stretched herself and got quietly out of bed. Oliver was still asleep; as his alarm was not due to go off for forty-five minutes.

By the time Jane had fed the dogs, the water was bubbling in the saucepan ready for the special heat-resistant individual rubber egg poaching cups. Oliver's alarm had gone off ten minutes earlier, so she only had to wait until he'd finished in the shower before putting the eggs on and then grilling the home-grown tomatoes.

This is the least I can do for Oliver after such a lovely dinner last night.

"My...my...my! This is a nice surprise, my love!"

"Take a seat, Sir," said Jane with a big grin, handing across Oliver's breakfast of toast with two perfectly poached eggs, and grilled tomatoes. "Enjoy!" She served her own dish and joined him.

"I didn't want you to think I'd forgotten how to cook," she grinned.

"Yum, this is a perfect start to the day. Thanks for cooking. I could smell it when I was under the shower, and my tummy started to rumble in anticipation."

They sat in silence, enjoying their home-grown vegetable and eggs from their small hen brood.

"Jane, I've decided to ask Jenny some different questions. Based firstly on the fact that she seems to know that it's her new heart that is giving her these weird dreams, and secondly that we know that Vicki Polites' heart is in her. Hopefully I might get some more information from her. This will also help her to eventually get back to a normal life. Mind you, I'm hoping that I might be able to get some more information for your case too."

"Thanks Oliver. I think we'll need any information we can get at the moment, because it looks as though one set of prints and DNA does not belong to either of Vicki's parents nor Loretta, which means they must belong to Vicki's murderer! I need to solve this case by conventional policing, with facts and scientific evidence that will help to convict the killer in court, and give eventual justice for the grieving family."

She looked at her watch.

"Jane, I'll clean up, you obviously want to go to work early today."

"Yes, I do. Thanks Oliver, what would I do without you?" She rushed out of the kitchen, grabbed her gear and returned to give Olive a quick kiss.

Three minutes later, she drove to the front gate, got out, closed it, and then drove her car towards the Calder highway and onto Melbourne.

Jane's team also arrived early, and they sat in the conference room, talking about the previous day's evidence.

Doctor Fred Harvey, had set up his usual slide show to emphasise his findings.

"As you can see in the first slide," he began once Jane arrived, "the fingerprints match Vicki's mother's prints on the adjacent slide," he switched to the next slide, "And these ones match her father's prints',' He continued, "The next two slides show matches with Loretta Stevens. And I'll now show you the interesting part of my analysis." Fred put up two more slides. "These prints don't match anyone who has been in Vicki's room that we know of. On these next slides, you'll see the DNA samples taken yesterday from Vicki's parents, and Loretta, which all match... *But*...voila, this sample of DNA belongs, I suspect, to the unidentified stranger. The main weird thing is that the non-matching DNA has some close comparisons with Vicki's mother!"

Jane was the first to react.

"So you're saying the unidentified fingerprints and DNA belong to someone closely related to Janet Polites?"

"In a nut shell, yes, close enough to be, for example a daughter or son."

"But Fred, as far as we know, Vicki was an only child," Angela asked, "And if it doesn't match John Polites, perhaps there's a previous child who visited Vicki's room?"

Fred nodded his head. "Yes, that is one explanation...possibly the most obvious...because the chances of a complete stranger having such comparable DNA would be almost impossible, I reckon."

Jane then added, "I think we will organise some formal interviews with the Polites. This way we might find out if there's a skeleton in the cupboard!" Her eyes were wide and she smiled. "I had another exchange of information with Steve Ho late yesterday. His murder case and our cold case now seem to be definitely connected via the common denominators; namely Loretta Stevens and her boyfriend, Pierre de Jong, who happens to be the son of his murder victim."

"The lying little bitch!" remarked Stan, his face now flushed as he flicked through his notes. "Yes, here it is...in our interview, she only casually mentioned meeting the Polites via nightclub friends, called, quote, Peter or Pierre and some other guy called Gray or Graham at a nightclub...both ex Melbourne Grammar boys...which obviously impressed her ladyship!"

"My reaction exactly, Stan," said Jane, "Steve Ho is interviewing Pierre de Jong again today, and is going to try and find out more about their relationship, and if possible something about his old school chum, Gray or Graham. The fact is, we now have copies of the transcripts of Ho's interviews with Loretta and the original one with Pierre. I'd like you to listen to each again, as we are now sharing as much information as possible with Ho's Special Crime Squad."

"Boss?"

"Yes, Angel?"

"As these cases are now connected, would it be possible to get copies of the other interviews from Steve's case? Before you ask why... I'll explain. Steve's victim was getting threats because of his public campaign about illegal transplant organs and tissues on the market in Australia. Our victim was an organ donor; plus Professor de Jong's senior theatre nurse, Susan Grant, is also nervous because of her close personal relationship with the late transplant surgeon; and our Vicki's parents have also admitted that they had threatening letters. I have a gut feeling that the transplant part of both cases could be connected, mainly through the illegal behind the scenes activity." Angela shrugged her shoulders and added, "Well that's my two cents worth, anyway."

Jane smiled at her, nodding, "Angel, you don't say much but when you do... That's why you're in this squad. I think we should definitely interview the Polites again, but this time in our office...separately...so that we might just get some idea of who might have been threatening them, and why. Then we could have a genuine motive of revenge and murder. Steve did tell me that Susan Grant was a terrific interviewee, with good background information about the de Jong family. As Pierre seems to be so involved with Loretta Stevens, the Ho Squad interviews could give us some valuable insights into these people in relation to our case. Well done, Angel. You've given us some valuable possible leads to work on."

Stan stopped sucking his pen and added,

"Boss, while we're talking about interviews, how about Doctor Aaron Browne, the head of the Melbourne Central Morgue, and Doctor Henry Stapleton, the former head, who's now running his own funeral parlour...bit weird, I think, especially as there are rumours at the Melbourne Central Hospital about *moonlighting* after hours!"

"Good point, Bluey! Agreed. Let's set up the sharing of interviews, and even new interviews with these people, if needed. Good brainstorming, everyone. I really feel we are getting on the right track to finding out the motives behind Vicki's death."

Jane picked up her satchel, indicating that the meeting was over.

"Let's get to work. We can swap information at the end of the day."

As she left the room, laughter broke out behind her. She turned to see a red-faced Angela, giggling, and saying, "Okay, Bluey, it was me this time, spilling something on the table, not you!" She went to the kitchenette for a paper towel.

Fred Harvey walked out with Jane.

"You know my dear, you have a first-class squad in there. I like to see good teamwork, and they really respect you too. Well done!" He patted her on the shoulder. "Well, I'm off to recheck those DNA results between Janet Polites and the mysterious person... just in case I missed something else. I'll let you know."

Ho sat with Charlie Chan and watched Pierre de Jong, sitting across from them, fidgeting nervously. His lips pouted, hands clenched in front of him on the table, and he asked, "What else do you want to know? I'm meant to be doing a special job for Melbourne Central Hospital. People's lives depend upon my programs..."

"IT programs, I presume? You're into IT stuff I believe," interjected Chan.

Pierre's face started to flush and slight beads of perspiration appeared on his upper lip as he responded. "Um, yes I'm doing a part-time course at RMIT in programming. It's much better than the medical studies at Melbourne Uni...my dad forced me into that course, and I hated it!"

Ho leaned forward in his seat and stared into Pierre's eyes. "I have information from RMIT that you failed last year, and were expelled due to bad behaviour and work."

"What?" Pierre's eyes, widened. "Why are you prying into my private life? It's none of your business what happened to me."

Ho smiled, "Because your father was murdered, it makes it okay for us to delve into your affairs, especially as you're so *anti* your father, mate. Now, let's get to the point. You also escaped with a cautionary sentence from a Magistrate a couple of years ago for forging your father's signature on a couple of cheques and documents. Tell us about that part of your private life."

Pierre's head dropped to his chest and he sighed. "Okay, you've got me there. The old fart wouldn't lend me money, so I got it anyway, but he dobbed me into the police, said it would be the best way to teach me a lesson as I wasn't going to listen to him. He was jealous of the fact that I have a talent to copy things...." He stopped mid-sentence, looking angry.

"I...I...um...that's why I like my IT work, creating webpages and documents..."

Charlie cleared his throat, and said, "You also run a private business from home which is connected with the paperwork requests and acquisitions of organ tissues for burns victims. Am I correct?"

"I...um...err...sort of!" Pierre glowered at Chan.

Chan then slammed his fist on the table. "Sort of? Bullshit! You're connected with something illegal, mate. You've had a cautionary sentence for forging. You also do part time work with Dr Henry Stapleton at the funeral home. Are you involved with something illegal with the funeral parlour? I can smell your fear across this table!"

Pierre shrank further into his chair. Beads of perspiration started to trickle down his neck and he pulled out his hanky. "I...I...I...um, I help Dr Stapleton with his paperwork. That's all! I don't know what else he does in the funeral home."

Ho tapped his pen on the table as he spoke. "Pierre, tell us about that paperwork. Are you using your forging skills for signatures?"

"What? I...oh shit, I'm in trouble, aren't I?"

Charlie nodded and said, "You certainly are, mate, but I don't think it involves the murder of your father. I think you've been used to help in the paperwork behind illegal tissue collection. Do you have any copies of this paperwork on your PC or anywhere else? It could help us to find the murderer."

Ho added, "Pierre, you're still in trouble with the law for forging, again, and I have to caution you at this point. However, anything you can tell us, anything at all about the signatories' names that you forged on the paperwork could count in your favour in court."

Pierre sat silent for a moment, sighed and looked at the two police officers and then said, "Okay...where shall I begin?"

Two hours later, Ho knocked on Jane's conference office door.

"Come in!" she called out.

Ho appeared, sporting a huge grin.

Jane grinned back at him and said, "You look like a cat that has swallowed a canary, Steve." She pointed to the coffee machine in the kitchenette. "Grab a coffee, take a seat and tell us all the good news."

Steve did just that. As he sat, he took a sip of his hot drink. "We have a bit of a break-through. Pierre has coughed up some vital information about an illegal group forging paperwork in order to collect tissues of dead people for use in hospitals. As far as the hospitals are concerned, everything is signed correctly by the consenting families. Pierre thinks the tissues are collected after hours in the hospital morgue, before the bodies are taken to the funeral home. Obviously, he can't prove it, but I think he's right. Pierre's only interested in the money he gets. He gets well paid for his clandestine work...as long as no questions are asked."

"Steve, what about his girlfriend, Loretta?" Jane paused, and then smiled. "Ah! Wait...So Loretta came onto Pierre for a while...especially after he got a precautionary sentence without conviction for forging his father's signature on cheques and important documents, which guaranteed Pierre's greed for the dollar and silence. He was a perfect candidate and background for the hospital paperwork forging. That *is* great news!"

Angela looked at Steve. "So Loretta's been using him to help her buddies? Hmmm, quite a bitch, this lady, isn't she? So she's probably involved with De Jong's murder, but not our Vicki's murder."

Ho smiled at his wife. "Yes, Angel, you're spot on there. By the way folks, Pierre says that he thinks Loretta moonlights at the hospital morgue some nights with Dr Stapleton. She has occasionally gone out late at night, but not to babysit, because it's too late...say around 2 am. She returns around 5 am, and then goes onto her shift at the hospital after a shower and change. A regular night owl! Oh, I asked about Graham. Pierre said he hasn't seen him for a couple of years, since their nightclubbing days with Loretta!"

Jane nodded her head at Steve. "Well, it looks like you may have found the right connection to solving your murder. Good luck with your interviews. Angel pointed out the fact that our victim's parents also received some threats. We're going to interview the Polites separately this afternoon, hopefully to see if they can tell us how the threats were made and by whom."

Steve Ho responded, "Ah! They were friendly with de Jong because of his campaign about illegal organs and tissues...right?"

Jane put a thumb up towards Ho. "Yep! Exactly! But I think our murderer is someone that the family knows. I don't know who or why yet, but we're going to give it a good go. That's why we'd like to go through your interviews with Dr Aaron Browne, Susan Grant and Dr Stapleton and of course, Loretta Stevens. Dr Stapleton organised Vicki's funeral. In fact I think we'll also interview Susan Grant ourselves."

Ho shook his head. "Hell, everything seems to be connected, except for the murderers. I tend to agree, Jane. Our murderers or murderer killed to try to stop de Jong finding out the truth behind the bad tissue donations on the market. I think he was getting too close."

Stan stopped picking some spilled biscuit off his shirt and said, "you're not wrong there Steve. Somewhere, there's someone in the Polites family who has a reason to kill an innocent young girl. Revenge? Hate? Possibly. I for one would be only too happy to delve into their lives...discreetly, mind you."

Jane smiled at Stan. "Your background in the traffic squad is paying off!"

The brainstorming session ended after Ho left the group and returned to his own squad. Jane then prepared her team for the interviews with the Polites, scheduled after their lunch break, and phoned Dr Fred Harvey.

"Fred? I've for a little job for you while you're at the State Morgue today. Could you try and find out any gossip about Dr Aaron Browne, but more in particular, Dr Henry Stapleton?"

Jane then briefly filled in Fred on the morning updates from Ho and how the two cases were now more intertwined.

Fred responded, "No problem, lovely lady. I won't get anything on Aaron...he's as straight as an arrow; squeaky clean. But Henry's another kettle of fish. Don't particularly like the man...difficult to work with and has a dark side to him. It will be a pleasure. I'll come back to you as soon as I discreetly can. I don't want to ruffle any feathers unnecessarily around here. I'm still working in their building, girl. Speak to you soon!"

Janet Polites was interviewed first. She sat down in front of Jane, clutched at her pink scarf, and then twisted her wedding ring around her finger. At intervals, she flicked her long blond hair from around her face.

Jane smiled at her. "Thanks for coming in today, Janet."

Janet's voice was very quiet. "Hopefully I can help you with some information. What would you like to know?"

Jane smiled at her. "We're interested in the threats that you received the weeks before Vicki died. Can you tell us what the threats were? And also how they were made?"

Janet's voice became stronger as she replied. "The threats were weird. They came in a plain envelope...no stamp...so obviously hand delivered when we weren't home. They were each in our letter box when we got home. The government security people checked them. They said that they were done on a PC. They still have them, if you need them."

"Janet, what sort of things did the notes say?" Angel asked.

Janet's eyes started to water. A tear ran down her cheek. Her lips trembled slightly as she replied. "The first simply said *I know something about you.* The second, *you don't know everything about me.* Then a third said *you'll pay for what you've done!* And that was all...just three threats in our mail box in three days...about two weeks before...before..." Janet burst into tears.

Jane touched Janet's hand and said, "Janet, Angela will take you to the café for a cup of tea. That's all we need to know for now. Again, thanks for coming in."

Jane then whispered to Angel, "Her husband is coming in for his interview in about an hour, so she needs to be gone before then. I don't want them to talk to each other until they see each other tonight at home."

"Gotcha, Boss," whispered Angela. She then ushered Janet Polites out of the office.

An hour later, John Polites' tall frame entered the interview room of the Special Case Squad. His snow-white teeth gleamed in the artificial lighting of the office against his dark, olive complexion. He shook the Detective Chief Superintendent's hand, "I hope everything is going well with your enquiry, Jane. I'm a bit busy in Parliament at the moment, so I can't be too long. At the same time, I'm only too willing to try and help you." He sat down opposite Jane, flashed another toothy grin at her, and added, "Sorry to hold you up...shall we proceed?"

Jane smile back and said, "We are interested specifically in the threats that you received before your daughter's death."

John shifted forward in his chair, a frown instantly formed on his forehead, "Oh yes...not a nice feeling at all, getting them. We received just three threats, three days running in our mail box. They were all sent to my wife, Janet. The first one said 'I know something about you' nothing else, but those words, I tell you, they'll haunt me for the rest of my life. Our whole world was turned upside down from that moment on."

"The second note?" prompted Jane.

"The second one was rather weird. It simply said, 'You don't know everything about me.' This of course really spooked us, as we naturally didn't know who the hell was sending these notes!" Polites clenched his fists. "The third day, the third note arrived, and this one was rather terrifying in its barbaric simplicity, 'You'll pay for what you've done!' That was when I hit the Cabinet panic button, so to speak, as the notes...initially vague, like a lot of the weird letters politicians get at times from disgruntled constituents...had suddenly become a direct threat upon my family and possibly our lives. So I called Government security services. They came very quickly to view the notes. Neither of us knew what the notes were referring to at all. We didn't have the foggiest! Obviously, someone with a gripe against Jane or maybe me, because I'm married to her, and the best way to hurt me would be to threaten her? I don't know who though...as an MP you tend to get people, sometimes supporters of the opposition who try and blame you for everything. I've never consciously hurt anyone in my life. Janet has certainly never hurt anyone."

Angela Nguyen gave John Polites a smile, and then asked quietly, "Mr Polites, is there someone in your family who possibly has misguided feelings against you, or your wife or daughter, and as a result, sent these threats to hurt the whole family? Can you think of any family upset or argument or dispute or history that could have caused this anger for revenge?"

John Polites shook his head slowly, his head bowed slightly as he thought quietly to himself for several minutes. "No...um, hold on, there's one thing I can think of, but..."

Jane looked at him and said quietly, "Please go on...this could be important, however trivial it might seem to you now."

"What I'm going to tell you is rather personal...well, very private information about my wife, Janet." He cleared his throat, and then continued, "As a teenager, long before we both met, Janet had a child out of wedlock. Her parents and the Church forced her to have the child adopted out straight after the birth. It must have been distressing for such a young girl at that time, she didn't even see the child at birth, the baby was simply taken away. Such was the culture at that time. It was shocking for her!"

Jane nodded her head, "Yes it would be dreadful at that age for her. Please go on, Mr Polites."

"Janet didn't even know if it was a girl or boy! Terrible things happened in those days. I still can't imagine how she felt or what she went through. Janet and I met years after. She, of course, told me that she wasn't a virgin, and why. The baby's father had disappeared as soon as he was told about her pregnancy. But I loved her...still do...so that little accident wasn't going to stop me marrying her. I didn't even tell my parents her tale, nor do Janet's parents know that I knew about Janet's baby. We kept it secret all these years."

Angela prompted, "So something happened to prompt your memory. Please tell us. This could be crucial to the enquiry on your daughter's death."

Polites took a deep breath and a sip of water before speaking. "Yes, you're right! Two months ago, we were contacted on the phone by a young man, a nineteen-year-old, who said his name was Graham Pappas. He said that he'd been told on his eighteenth birthday by his parents that he'd been adopted at birth. Apparently, the Pappas family already had six children. This lad wanted to meet his biological mother...who he believed was Janet! Our main concern was of course, Vicki. Suddenly having a half-brother in the picture made us hesitate. He asked to come a week later to meet us. We weren't sure, so we asked him to give us time to think about a suitable time to meet. He didn't seem that happy, but agreed to phone again in a week.

We didn't hear from him for two weeks, and then he finally contacted us again."

"Did that delay upset you?" asked Jane.

"Well yes, it upset me, but I didn't tell Janet that. I just wanted a peaceful relationship between all of us, so I organised a meeting the next day."

"Tell us about the meeting, John," probed Jane.

"Well, he arrived on time, I felt that was a plus in his favour. However, he didn't show much emotion. A quiet lad, a bit awkward. Mind you, it must have been a bit of a daunting experience for him to meet his biological mother. Oh, he did mention that he was a carpenter...a builder. He seemed genuinely keen to get to know us and wanted to meet Vicki, his half-sister, who was due home from school at that time. Funnily enough, during his short visit, he even helped me hang the painting in Vicki's room that we'd bought for her as a surprise. I must add that he was very polite and friendly, and was nice to Vicki when they finally met. He kept the painting secret when she took her schoolbag upstairs to her room, and suddenly returned, full of excitement at discovering the painting on her bedroom wall. It was a painting that she'd admired a few days earlier when we were walking past an antique shop. He was also kind towards Janet. I don't think he knew the full story behind the adoption...it wasn't the right time to ask, anyway. Weirdly, we haven't seen him since. He hasn't contacted us. Although, strangely enough, I did see him briefly at Vicki's funeral...and that was in the distance...and not since. By the way, I haven't told Janet about the funeral sighting. I didn't want to upset her further that day, or since. He doesn't answer any call either. I think he's still finding the fact that he was adopted out daunting. We don't even have a photo of him..." His voice trailed off. His head bowed. He suddenly looked up at the two detectives and then looked at his watch. "I'm sorry, I must go."

Jane responded, "That's all for now. I know you're busy. There's just one more thing."

"Yes? Anything I can do to help?"

"Please let me know if Graham contacts you or Janet again. Here's my card. Don't alarm your wife. We would just like to talk to Graham, if we're able." With Jane's words, the interview was over.

Stan greeted Jane and Angela as they emerged from the interview room. "The sandwiches have arrived from the canteen, coffee's ready to pour." He was wiping some spilt milk off the bench in the kitchenette, and grinned as he continued, "Yes, Angel, sorry but I knocked the milk carton on the bench... Well, did you learn anything new, Boss?"

Jane laughed, "You're a breath of fresh air, Bluey. We love you the way you are, so never apologise."

They joined Stan in the kitchenette and took their specifically labelled packet of food out of their boxes and onto a plate, grabbed a hot coffee each and returned into the conference room for a working lunch.

"To answer your question, Bluey, yes, we learned something very private, but extremely important for our investigation," remarked Jane as she started to eat her chicken and avocado sandwich. "Hmm, this is delicious! Okay, John Polites told us that Janet had a baby as a young teenager, which according to the culture of her society at that time, demanded that her baby be taken away from her as soon as it was born!"

"Hell, poor thing. I've read about this, Boss. What I'd call inhumane, to say the least. A bit like some folk putting tiny puppies into a sack and throwing them into a river because they don't want them!"

Jane nodded her head, "My sentiments entirely, Bluey. The most interesting fact is that the baby was taken as soon as it was born, and Janet didn't even know the sex of the poor thing. Polites also told us that Janet told him about this when they met and became an item. He said he loved her and that didn't matter to him as what happened to the baby was essentially out of her control."

Stan smiled, and said, "Seems like he's quite a guy, despite being a Pollie!"

Everyone laughed.

Jane continued. "The really interesting information is that two months ago, the Polites were contacted by a young man of nineteen, called Graham Pappas."

Bluey reacted immediately. "Bet you this is the Graham that Loretta was talking about!"

"We don't know that for a fact at the moment, but it's worth keeping in mind. Could be a coincidence too, Bluey...but I see your point." Jane winked at Stan. "My, Bluey can I see you blushing?"

"Aw heck, Boss, nope! Just feeling a little hot in here, that's all." Bluey then started on his second roast beef and gravy sandwich. "Damn, the gravy's just dribbled down my shirt!"

Jane continued with a smile as Bluey dabbed his shirt with his paper napkin.

"This Graham Pappas was adopted out to the Pappas family at birth. Apparently, they had six children already at the time, of their own. Obviously, part of the Greek community, who had decided to give the baby a home...and their name!"

"Did he meet the Polites' family?"

"Yes, eventually. He even met Vicki, and had helped John Polites to hang the painting on her bedroom wall."

"This is getting spooky, Boss. Graham is beginning to sound like a possible suspect."

"Angel and I agree, Bluey. The thing is, this guy has disappeared and never returned to visit the Polites family again..."

Angela interrupted, "But Polites spotted him at Vicki's funeral service...in the distance He never spoke to the family on that day."

"Yep, I knew it; he's a suspect, Boss. Angel and I should start to see if we can find him."

"Yes, that will be on our *to do list*, Bluey. But first, I want you to join me this afternoon in interviewing Sister Susan Grant."

"Now that will be a pleasure, Boss. Ho's team reckon she's one lovely lady."

An hour later, a buxom middle-aged lady with grey, short cropped hair came into the reception area in the foyer on the ground floor. She was sent up in the lift to the Special Cold Case Squad Office. Jane welcomed her.

"Thanks for coming in to see us, Susan. We really appreciate it. Please come in."

Jane ushered Susan Grant into the interview room. She introduced Stan Johnson, and-offered her a coffee, which was gratefully accepted.

Jane started the interview. "Susan, we've asked to talk to you because you work at the Melbourne Central Hospital in the theatre, and assist in transplant surgery there."

"That's correct."

"You worked with Loretta Stevens and Professor de Jong?" prompted Jane.

"Yes, in fact, I often swapped places with Sister Loretta Stevens, when she wasn't available. I...I worked closely with Johann, but you know that already."

"Yes, we do, Susan. What we need to know in our case involving Vicki Polites, is if anything was unusual about her operation?"

"Vicki? So you're investigating her death? I thought you were somehow involved with Johann's death... I thought Vicki died in an accidental fall at home!" Susan sighed, and then added, "Hell, I guess not, or you wouldn't be asking me questions. What has changed in Vicki's death?"

Stan then intervened. "Susan, her parents asked for another autopsy. It was granted and the findings are that she had bruising on her neck and arms, which are not compatible with an accidental fall down the staircase."

Susan's eyes opened wide. "Oh no, so did Loretta hear or see anyone? She was at the house at the time..."

"No," replied Stan. "It appears the noise of the fall and a scream woke Loretta. She says that she was groggy...could have been drugged...but was able to apply CPR and call for an ambulance."

"Okay, what do you want to know? Do you mean before or during or after the transplant?"

Jane smiled at Susan and said, "Hmmm, well firstly, Vicki was on life support when she was at hospital to keep her alive whilst two senior doctors checked to see if her tissue matches could help anyone in a transplant. Her parents, naturally distraught, were counselled; and I believe eventually signed paperwork giving consent. Then we believe Vicki was kept on the life support during that night, so that organs could be collected from her. So they operated on her that night?"

"No. The next morning. All those on duty were tired after a long day in theatre. Also, senior staff needed to find the right recipients, who might be in Melbourne or interstate. It takes time to set up multiple transplants. Life support is so crucial in this situation. I'm used to this, of course. It's my job. It's so hard on the donor's family when their loved one is clinically dead, but still breathes because of the machinery, which keeps oxygen and blood flowing through the organs. The thing that keeps them going at that time is the hope that other people and their families have hope. That's what I keep telling them, anyway. It seems to help."

Steve's right, Susan's a terrific witness. She remembers every detail. Just what we want. She's a compassionate lady too. I like you, Susan Grant.

Susan continued. "Doctor Chan and Loretta and I were going off duty that night after some simple general surgery, and obviously were going to be required, the next day once a recipient was available in Melbourne. We're transplant nursing theatre specialists. Transplants don't exactly happen every day, as you know."

"So the next day, you assisted Professor Johann de Jong?" asked Jane.

"Yes, along with Loretta. Dr Chan, the senior general surgeon, was in the adjacent theatre, retrieving Vicki's heart for our Melbourne based patient."

"Jenny Summers..." said Jane.

Susan gasped. "How did you know?"

"Sorry, Susan, but it was the only heart transplant in the hospital that day. It was also the day after Vicki Polites was injured, and resuscitated by her babysitter, Loretta. We're not advertising this information, however."

"You're right, of course, Chief Superintendent."

"Please, call me Jane. This is an informal interview, Susan. We need the insight of someone like you."

"I understand, Jane. To tell you the truth, I've always been uncomfortable in the fact the Loretta was babysitting for the Polites. After all, she was also doing extra night work. You probably know the gossip already...moonlighting in the hospital morgue the last few years, then recently at Dr Henry Stapleton's funeral parlour. Supposedly as a makeup artist of all things! Sorry, but I don't personally like Loretta, mainly because I feel she stretches herself too far professionally. I also think that she's close to being unethical, if you know what I mean." She shrugged her shoulders.

Stan nodded at Susan and said, "This is exactly the information we need Susan. Please go on."

"Sorry, I'd better make myself clear. Dr Johann de Jong and I were very close friends, in fact, intimately...but we never, ever brought our personal lives into the hospital environment. We were very discrete. It's not against the rules to have relationships in our work environment. It happens a lot actually. Johann was very passionate about the quality of the heart transplant work that he did, as well as other heart operations. Hence the campaign of his...which I think led eventually to his demise! I think someone knew he was getting too close to the illegal tissue collection game that was going on."

Jane and Stan let Susan continue at her own pace and calmly watched her sip her coffee, before she continued. "Sorry, I'm digressing."

Jane smiled at her and said, "Not at all, Susan. You're giving us valuable insight and information for our case. Please go on. For instance...can you tell us about the relationship between Pierre de Jong and Loretta?"

"Oh, regarding Pierre's relationship with Loretta...I reckon it's one sided. I don't think Loretta really gives a toss about him or anyone else for that matter. She's too self-centred. Well, as you probably know, Johann's wife died a few years ago in childbirth. Pierre was furious that she'd even got pregnant...basically blaming his father for her death and went off the rails a bit. He deliberately flunked his first year of medicine at Melbourne University. Then he turned to R.M.I.T Uni as a part time IT student, and at the same time helping Dr Stapleton with documentation. I honestly feel, but can't prove it, of course, that he could have been involved in the suspected illegal documentation discovered in tissue transplants within Australia, but the courts couldn't prove anything of course. Pierre's a clever forger of signatures, but you know that...it's on the police records." Susan sighed, and ran her hand through her short cropped hair. "His father did so much for him, but Pierre never showed that he was grateful...quite the opposite!"

Stan then spoke. "Yes, we do know about Pierre's suspended sentence, but it's interesting that you think he's involved in the illegal work that his father was so against. We'll take careful note of that insight. Thanks, Susan."

Susan raised her eyebrows. "For Detective Inspector Steve Ho's case? That's good. I reckon the two cases are connected in some way. But that's your job. I'm only a theatre nurse."

Jane said, "And a good one, from what we've heard. Are you worried about your safety at all? I'm asking because of your closeness to Professor Johann de Jong."

"Yes...but only a little. I'm keeping a low profile at work. I'm in a secure unit with an alarm..."

Jane handed Susan her business card. "Please let us know if you need any help, Susan, anytime. We won't be advertising what you've told us today, that's for sure. Your information has given us very important background insight. Thank you so much for coming in today, on your day off, too! Oh, one more question, if I may. Have you ever heard of a Graham Pappas?"

"No, sorry, never heard of him." Susan shook both Jane and Stan's hands firmly. "I'll contact you if I think of anything else that might help you find Vicki's killer...or if I need any help. Thanks for the offer, by the way, it's appreciated."

As Susan left the office, Stan grinned, "She's quite a lovely lady, Boss!"

Jane's team met for a briefing to collect updates from the day's interviews.

"Thanks for the good work today, everyone," said Jane. "We've gained further insight into the backgrounds of the Polites family, and also the de Jong family from Janet and John Polites and then Susan Grant's interviews. Any comments?"

Stan was the first to respond. "I'd like to find this mysterious Graham Pappas, Boss."

"That's if we can trace him, Stan," replied Angela, "because from what the John Polites said, he seems to have vanished, and is not responding to any calls either."

At that moment, Dr Fred Harvey entered the conference room.

"Afternoon all! I'm glad I caught you before you disappeared for the day. I have some gossip to report to you on Dr Stapleton and Loretta Stevens, which I know will be of great interest."

"The floor is yours, Doc. We're all ears," said Jane.

"It's not much, but enough to say that firstly Dr Henry Stapleton left Melbourne Central Hospital under a slight smoke screen...not really a cloud. He basically resigned before he was sacked. The board had heard rumours that he was spending too much time in the hospital morgue without collecting overtime in pay. It was also said that he used a staff member to help, but never confided who that person was. It was all rather hush-hush."

Jane leaned forward on the table and said, "Loretta Stevens?"

"That's the common theory. But there's no concrete evidence in records or payroll notes. The gossip also is that it's strange that he's gone from dissecting and inspecting dead bodies, to patching up and making up bodies for burial or cremation. Um, the words used were, *Henry just likes to play with the dead!*"

"Anything else, Fred?" asked Jane.

"Nope, sorry. If I pried any further, it would have been obvious that I was pumping for inside info, which I don't honestly believe anyone that knew the man would know. I only knew him briefly from the times he visited the State Mortuary. Even then, Dr Stapleton was a bit of a weirdo who kept to himself. But underneath, I reckon he was a pretty cunning businessman. Look how successful he's been since he left the hospital. Strangely, the hospital hierarchy must have short memories, or there's been a change in management since he worked there and his suspect exit from their employ a few years ago, because the hospital is now happy to have him collect bodies from their morgue to take to his funeral parlour." Fred then took a long drink of his coffee, and then added, "That's all I've got for you folks. How's the cold case going?"

"Going well, mate. Feel free to listen and watch the interviews we did today with Janet and John Polites and Susan Grant," replied Jane.

"Thanks, Jane, but I'll look at them tomorrow morning. It's home time," he replied, looking at his watch. It was about that time for Jane and her team, too.

Jane relaxed at home with Oliver in the lounge. With Sassy and Spunky lying near their feet on a large sheepskin rug, snoring gently, Jane told Oliver all her news.

"You're getting somewhere, Jane. I'm so proud of you!" He gently kissed her.

Jane whispered, "Don't wake up the dogs," she giggled.

"Well, my news is that Jenny seemed much better today. She didn't really add much more of interest to yesterday's chat, except that she kept repeating stuff about the dark figure, the painting, and the fall." He sighed and added, "Unlike you, I don't seem to be getting far on my case. But at least Jenny's more relaxed with me."

"Good, that means she trusts you. Oliver, I have a weird request."

"Oh?"

"You can say no...but, can I sit in on the chat you have with Jenny tomorrow morning? I can take some time from work, as it's mainly paperwork. I won't say anything, I promise."

"Why do you want to meet Jenny?"

"I'm hoping to see Vicki's ghost...maybe her ghost will recognise me from my visit to her parents' house, and try to contact me direct, outside your office...say in the park? I could go outside for a short break, while you keep talking to Jenny. What do you think?"

"Jane, I should say no, but in this instance, I could tell Jenny that you're a colleague, interested in her case that I'm co-ordinating with. Hmm, Okay...alright!"

"You're a gem, Oliver Tarrant!" Jane gave him a long, lingering kiss. "Mmm, it's time for bed, mate."

Day Five

After walking Sassy and Spunky around the paddocks early the next morning, Jane and Oliver had a breakfast of scrambled eggs collected from their hens' shed.

"Golly, I just love our own eggs, Oliver. They're far better than the ones you can buy in the shops. By the way, I really appreciate you trusting me to see Jenny this morning. I've contacted the office and advised them that I'm going to be in late."

"Mmm, you're not wrong...these eggs are delicious!" Oliver swallowed his last mouthful and drank his orange juice. "Perhaps we should put an orange tree in the nearby paddock, near the lemon and lime trees. Then we can also have freshly squeezed juice each morning. Jane, do you really think the ghost of Vicki will appear to you again?"

"I hope so. I just have a feeling that she might, especially as she's apparently haunting Jenny's new heart at the moment." Jane paused for a brief moment, then added, "Yes, Jenny's *Haunted Heart!* Hopefully, Vicki will see me in the room... Well fingers crossed! She could tell me so much...that's of course if she's a talking ghost like the other ghosts of my past cases. "

Oliver and Jane cleared the table, stacked the dishwasher, and got ready to leave for the day.

"Oliver, I'll follow you. Brr! It's a real autumn day today."

"Yep! We need the rain after all the hot summer. We've had to rotate the alpacas around the paddock more than usual this year, because of the lack of new grass."

"I love our hobby farm, Oliver. When we both retire, it will still keep us active and provide a nice income for our old age."

Oliver laughed. "We're not old enough to retire yet, my love." He wrapped his scarf around his neck. "Mind you, the alpacas certainly provided a nice wool clip this year. The local spinning mill had a field day, making knitted and woven items."

"Yes, Nancy was able to sell the sweaters, hats, gloves, scarves and socks very quickly. They couldn't keep up with the demand."

"We're lucky to have such good neighbours who know the alpaca business, and have taught us so much."

They drove out in separate cars, and headed south to Moonee Ponds, where Oliver had his consultancy in an office building next to a lovely park. It was not far from the end of the famous Puckle Street, often mentioned by Barry Humphries' famous character, Dame Edna Everidge. Jane planned to travel further on to St. Kilda to her office after the meeting with Jenny Summers.

Jane smiled as Jenny Summers entered Oliver's consulting room. *Yes, just like her photo, with beautiful clear blue eyes, fair skin and what lovely ginger hair!*

"Hello, Jenny. Please make yourself comfortable." He gestured to Jane, who was seated on another arm chair on the other side of the room. "This is a colleague of mine. Her name is Jane. She does similar work to me, and I've invited her to come and meet you today."

"Hello, Jenny. I already feel that I know you. I'm glad to meet you at last. Would you like a homemade shortbread?" Jane took a plate of biscuits over to Jenny, who picked up one.

"Go on...take two, I have two on my plate over there," grinned Jane.

"Yum. Thanks, Jane." The girl smiled before blurting, "Do you know about my nightmares?"

"Yes I do, Jenny. Oliver has told me about them. I'm going to sit over there and listen to you two for a while."

"That's okay," Jenny responded with a smile.

Jane sat down again, her mind racing with thoughts. *Oliver...fancy saying I do similar work to you! Heck, I know that I've got a degree in Psychology and criminology and an MBA in criminology, but I'm certainly not a Professor of Psychology, like you. Then again, we both have studied Psychology, so I won't be entirely out of my depth here... I hope!*

Oliver started the session with Jenny. "Well, Jenny, have you had any other dreams since we last met?"

"Just the same ones...but not as often."

Jane was still silent, but thought to herself. *Darn it! On the one hand, I want this lovely kid cured, and on the other hand, I want her to have a clearer image of the heart's original owner's murderer!* She still remained silent, letting Oliver do the questioning.

"Are you still seeing the dark intruder in the room in your dream?"

"Yeah. Last night, I saw his hairy arm with blond hair."

"How could you see this in the dark of your room?"

"It wasn't that dark, it was fairly light, because there was a night light on the desk. I forgot about that before. Weird, 'cause my bedroom at home is darker at night! I... I...know that my dreams are not about my house, Oliver.

It's weird. It's like I'm another person when I dream!" Jane noticed that Jenny's eyes were now wide open as she spoke.

You are another person, Jenny when you dream, you're Vicki. Oh, you poor kid! I hope we can help you. Hell, I'm beginning to think that the only way will be for me to find Vicki's killer.

Jane turned her attention to Jenny's Pooh Bear Teddy that she was holding onto tightly as she spoke. Oliver nodded at Jane to go ahead and talk to Jenny.

"What do you call your teddy, Jenny?"

"Pooh!" She grinned.

"Good name. I had a fluffy, shaggy teddy when I was your age. He was my best friend, especially when I was happy or scared. We shared everything together, even stuff that I didn't tell my mum or dad."

"What was his name?"

"Teddy...yep that sounds pretty dumb now, but I loved him. I still love him. I have him on the dressing table back home."

"That's nice. I'm going to keep Pooh until I'm as old as you. That's a neat idea!"

Jane suddenly felt like an old woman. She grinned at Jenny and responded, "I'm not ancient yet, Jenny. Mind you, I feel like it sometimes."

Jenny laughed. Oliver leaned forward and offered Jenny more shortbread. Jane stroked her nose until Oliver noticed. It was a prearranged signal that she had organised with him to let him know that she could see the ghost of Vicki in the room with them, visible to only Jane.

Jane quietly stood up and said, "Sorry, but I need to go to my car. I've forgotten my mobile, and my work might want to contact me. I shan't be long."

Oliver winked at Jane as she left the room.

Jane was finding it hard to breathe. She pulled out her inhaler for her asthma, and had two quick doses. She deliberately walked casually out of the old Victorian Villa building. She waited until she crossed the road and walked into the park before turning toward the ghostly figure of Vicki Polites, who was following her. *Just like my other ghosts; no shadow, semitransparent...it's ethereal!*

"Hello, Vicki. It's nice to see you again. Would you like to sit with me under the tree there, on the park bench?"

Please talk to me, Vicki!

"Okay."

The voice was almost a whisper. They sat down together, and Jane said quietly, "I don't want to be away from Oliver and Jenny for too long. Jenny might get suspicious that I'm doing something else other than getting my mobile."

"Which you already have on you," giggled Vicki. "Thank you for being able to see me. You've seen ghosts before, haven't you?"

"Yes, but don't tell anyone, will you."

"Oliver knows, and I know he's your husband. I've followed you to your lovely farm a few times. The first time was after I first saw you at my house. I love those white animals. What are they called?"

"Alpacas. We shear them once a year for their woolly coats to weave at the local mill into lovely garments which are sold at the local market."

"Yes, I heard you talking about that this morning."

Heck, what else has this girl heard?

Vicki continued, "You're investigating my murder. I know because you're a Detective Chief Superintendent of the Special Cold Case Squad. That's what you told mum and dad when you came to our house the day I first saw you in my bedroom."

"Yes, Vicki, you're right. I'm sorry I didn't get time to chat with you then."

"Yeah, mum came in. I didn't want to scare her...I feel so weird, I can't be seen except by you. I know mum and dad are so sad, I know I'm dead, but I'm inside another person! How come?"

"When you died, your parents consented that the doctors could use your good organs to help other people, Vicki."

"Transplants!"

"Exactly."

"Hey, one of my school friends had a brother who got a new kidney from a dead donor. Wow! So some lucky people got help from me?"

"You should be proud of that fact, Vicki. There's research about how some recipients of organs, particularly of hearts, have images or experiences that only the former owner of the heart knew about."

"So Jenny has my heart, and that's where my soul is at the moment; and not gone to heaven. I heard the priest at my funeral talk about my soul! This is weird. I guess I'm a wandering ghost because I want someone...especially you...to find my killer, then I can finally rest!"

"Yes, I think you've described your situation very well, Vicki. You were very clever to use nightmares to get people's attention."

"Not deliberately...it just happened. I wanted everyone to know that it wasn't an accident. That person in my room was being nasty to my teddy, and to my painting on the wall. He said that I didn't deserve such nice things and that they should be shared, and the painting should be his!"

"Vicki, thanks for telling me this. It will help me find this person. You just said *he* again. Jenny keeps telling Oliver that the intruder whispered and she didn't know if it was male or female. Are you sure it was a man?"

"I wasn't before, but I am now. I've only just remembered his hairy arm. That came back when I was talking to you through Jenny's dreams. Thanks for helping me, Jane. I want to stop this weird state, I want peace. I know poor Jenny wants peace too, doesn't she?"

Jane nodded, "Yes, she does. It's my job to find concrete facts to present in court...to prove the man we catch is your murderer and is brought to justice. Then I know you and Jenny will be happy forever. How does that sound?"

"Good! You have to go back now?"

"Yes, I do. Promise me that until I catch this evil man, you'll contact me in the evening, when I get home? We can catch up on things. I need your help to guide me to get this evidence I need. Eventually, Vicki, you'll be at peace."

"Okay, but will you promise me something in return?"

"Yes, if I can...what do you want?"

"I'd like you to give Harry to Jenny."

"Harry?"

"My teddy that you cuddled that day you came into my room and saw me on the bed. Harry and Pooh can sit next to each other on her desk. Then I'll be at peace, with my best friend and the same room as Jenny's best friend, while my heart beats on inside her!"

"I just wish I could hug you, Vicki Polites. You're such a lovely person...err...ghost!"

The odd couple got up and returned to the consulting rooms.

Jane finally left Oliver's consulting room half an hour later, after Jenny's mother had collected her daughter.

"I'll see you later, Oliver."

"I look forward to then, my love," he replied, and kissed her briefly before his next patient came in.

Jane was full of mixed emotions as she drove south through the city traffic towards the St. Kilda police building.

Now I know we're looking for a male. Possibly a natural blond, because of the hair Vicki saw on the arm. What a lovely girl, Vicki was. No wonder her mother is a mess! Heck, I was a mess when we lost our little Amy. That's over five years ago, now. I'm so lucky to have Oliver, the hobby farm and of course our lovely Sassy and Spunky, and Alpacas...our four-legged children!

Jane parked in her designated parking spot under the building. She went up in the lift to the ground floor and straight to the café. A familiar voice spoke from behind her as she waited in the queue to collect her coffee.

"You're late this morning, Jane."

Jane spun around. "Hi Steve. Yes, I stayed home to finish some paperwork, before I came here," she lied.

"Okay, let's have a chat while we have our coffees, shall we?"

"How are my beautiful god-children, Kylie and Khan going at school?"

"They love it, Jane. They're both very mature five-year-olds. Full of energy and enthusiasm, all the time too. Kylie loves her dolls and Khan is currently mad on train spotting."

"We must catch up with them sometime, soon, Steve."

"What about next weekend...say Saturday?"

"Darn it! Oliver has a special clinic on Saturday, but Sunday is okay with us. How about bringing the kids to our farm to see the Alpacas, and the dogs, of course. They can help to wear out Sassy and Spunky for us."

"That's a promise. Sunday it is. Khan, Kylie, Angel and I will be there with bells on. What time? Can we bring anything?"

Jane laughed, and then said, "Just bring the Ho family, and maybe a bottle of wine, if you like, say around eleven, then the kids can play before we have a barbeque lunch."

"Sounds great... Now tell me, why were you really late, this morning?"

Jane flicked her long auburn hair back from her face. "Heck, you know me only too well, Steve Ho." She leaned forward at their table and said quietly, "Between the two of us, I was sitting in on Oliver's patient chat this morning."

"Why?"

"It was Jenny Summers, the one who received my Vicki Polites' heart as a transplant!"

Ho lowered his voice almost to a whisper. "You've been communicating with a ghost again?"

"Yes. I first saw Vicki's ghost when I went into her bedroom the other day. Unfortunately, her mother, Janet Polites, came into the bedroom unexpectedly, and the ghost suddenly vanished. So last night, I thought that if I could see her again, I might just be able to talk to her. Mind you I didn't know if this ghost could talk to me at that time. The obvious place was Oliver's consulting rooms, in Moonee Ponds. I felt that it would be a perfect place to communicate with her, especially once she saw me through Jenny's eyes. I asked Oliver if I could sit in on his chat and he said yes. We organised a signal...basically me rubbing the side of my nose, as if in thought, the moment I could see Vicki's ghost!"

"And it happened? What about Jenny? A ghost would scare her silly..."

"Of course not, Steve. I was the only one who could see her ghost. You know me. At the pre-set signal, I made an excuse to go to my car next to the park for my *forgotten mobile*. Oliver pretended that this was normal and off I went, and thankfully the ghost of Vicki followed me to the park...and to my relief, actually talked to me."

Steve whispered, "Jane, this is fantastic! Your ethereal powers are still there. What a bonus in our profession! Hey, obviously I'll say nothing, as usual."

Jane then told him about her amazing experience, talking with the ghost for a good five minutes.

"Jane, I'm intrigued that you now know that the killer is a male. Now you've just got to find concrete evidence to nail him. Well done. Please keep me up to date with these special communications."

"I will. By the way, how's your case going?"

"Not badly at all. In fact, we've been able to exclude Dr Aaron Browne from our suspects. Pierre de Jong has an alibi too, which is crossed referenced with the alibi of Loretta Stevens. Remember, Sergeant Standing's squad found them together when they called at his flat to advise Pierre about his father's death."

"Hey, don't forget that Standing called in on them the morning after de Jong Senior was killed... You may need to recheck both their movements again, mate...um, sorry, I'm acting like your Boss again."

"Point taken Boss, I agree. I'll get Bah Bah to ask Jason Standing to double check their alibis."

"Are Mary and Jason becoming a pair? I've heard whispers around the corridors about them. If so, great. They make a nice couple."

Ho laughed, and responded, "Yes, a similar match, like Bluey and Sister Susan Grant."

"What?"

"Aha, got you there. Angel and I saw them together at Southbank, enjoying a drink together after work yesterday. Another good match methinks!"

Jane shook her head, "Do you realise that we're behaving like old surrogate parents, match-making our lonely squad members. We'd better leave them alone, to find their own destinies, eh?"

"Yes, mother hen!"

"Now, before I forget, have you made any further progress with Pierre and the forging?"

"Yes, Pierre had 'fessed up to doing illegal forging paperwork for Dr Henry Stapleton, which we'll hand over to the fraud squad after this case's evidence is finalised. It turns out he did work for Stapleton for the Melbourne Central Hospital morgue, as well as for his funeral parlour. He's been paid lots of money for this. He's a greedy little sod. Not a nice lad at all really...as you'd agree...but we need him as a special witness in our murder case first, at this stage."

"He's hoping that the courts will be more lenient with him because of information received?"

"Absolutely! We haven't really advised that this might not be the case...not yet, anyway...if he believes that, it's helping our enquiries." He winked at Jane. "Besides, I hate the little prick. I need his information to find out who else could have been involved in his father's death."

"I for one have a gut feeling that Loretta is involved. She's a good liar, and can spin a hefty yarn for self-protection."

Ho sighed. "Agreed. Taking in what you said about possible alibi discrepancies, she possibly had time to be with, say, Dr Stapleton to drug de Jong, assist in his murder, and then help move the body to Roxburgh Park, dump him in the lake and return to the so-called love nest to be with Pierre. He wouldn't have noticed, because he's into taking drugs, especially at home alone. What do you think?"

"Yep, I concur. I also don't think Pierre killed his father. He hated him, yes, because he blames his father for his mother's childbirth related death."

"Ah, yes...you've been talking to Susan Grant. Nice witness that one."

"What's Stapleton's alibi?"

"Not good. He reckons he was alone at the funeral parlour, doing paperwork."

"For what it's worth, I reckon Loretta was with him at the parlour at some time. I don't think she's in love with Pierre at all."

"Really?"

"Yes, really. I'll bet you she's only using Pierre for Stapleton and her own cause...namely making lot of money from frantic families needing paperwork for tissue donations for their sick ones."

"Do you know something, Jane?"

"What?"

"I know, I've said this before, but I miss working and brainstorming with you."

"But you *are* working with me, well at the moment we're co-ordinating information and ideas on our cases..."

Ho smiled at her and replied, "You know what I mean, Boss." He looked at his watch "I'd better get back to my office. Charlie and Bah Bah have been busy this morning with a warrant searching Stapleton's funeral parlour, including the out-shed. We're hoping that they'll find some incriminating evidence. They rang earlier to say they had surprised him completely with their visit. That's what we wanted to do."

"Well, we have a surname for our mystery Graham, Graham Pappas, who was the *lost* birth time adopted son of Janet Polites; an illegitimate child before she met and married John Polites. The Pappas family adopted him, despite already having six kids of their own. Unfortunately, we don't have any photos of Graham as yet. But he's actually met the Polites family. He was told about his adoption a year ago, and wanted to meet his biological mother...whom he did...a few weeks before Vicki's death!"

"So you too have a good murder suspect. Why don't you arrest him?"

"He's missing!"

"I'd suggest starting at the adoption office and working forward..."

"There you go...now you're sounding like my Boss, mate." She grinned. "That's what I intend to do this afternoon. See you soon?"

"Of course. Enjoy the rest of your day, Jane. Say G'day to Oliver."

Stan looked up at Jane as she entered the office.

"Must have been a lot of paperwork this morning, Boss."

"A fair bit," she lied, and then added, "I also bumped into Steve Ho downstairs, and we've been swapping notes on our updates for the last half hour." *Heck, why am I making excuses to my own squad? Maybe it's because I have this secret that I can communicate with ghosts. It's a weird thing for someone in charge of cold cases, I have to admit. At least I can confide in Steve and Oliver.*

Bluey smiled at her, "Well you're just in time for lunch." He pointed to three large pizza boxes on the conference table. "We were just waiting for you to come and join us. We have some information to share with you."

Jane peered into each box. "Yum! Vegetarian, chicken and Aussie style with eggs. One guess who's eating the Aussie one... Bluey...the vegetarian... Angel, and Moi...the chicken?"

"Got it right, Boss," said Angela who entered the room with cups of coffee on a tray.

"Alright everyone," said Jane. She continued as the squad entered the room, "Grab some paper serviettes and let's sit and talk shop!"

Angela flicked her long black hair and tied it into a ponytail, and then sipped some coffee before she spoke. "Boss, we took the liberty of doing some research about this Graham Pappas that John Polites told us about yesterday afternoon."

Stan swallowed the first mouthful of his Aussie pizza, and said, "Our first stop this morning was to the adoption records office. We flashed our ID's, which certainly seemed to impress the chick at the counter," he laughed, "she immediately got her supervisor to come to the desk to see us."

"Stan emphasised that we were from the Special Cold Case Squad, investigating the death of MP John Polites' daughter, Vicki Polites. And because of the recent publicity about her death in the papers and on TV, the records office obligingly gave us Graham Pappas' adoption file to research. They even gave us photocopies of the paperwork, and countersigned them as *official copies* to help us use them in court. The papers state the biological mother and the adoptive parents. Here's the evidence." Angela handed Jane their file.

Jane wiped her had on a napkin, before handling them, and quietly scanned them for a few minutes before responding. "So what John Polites told us is absolutely correct. Poor Janet didn't even know the baby's sex, let alone name. The little one didn't even get to be held by his mother! Janet didn't have any say at all, legally, because she was only fifteen years old at the time. Under the age of consent. Good work, you two!"

Bluey then brought forward more paperwork for Jane to see, saying, "We also looked up Graham Pappas in the directories, tax office files and rates files. His last known address was in a rented flat in Brunswick. He'd apparently left the Pappas family home shortly after his eighteenth birthday."

Jane responded, "That's after he was told that he was adopted, and not a blood member of the Pappas family. It must have had a huge impact on him."

Angela added, "I've contacted the Pappas family home in Essendon. Mrs Pappas was happy to give some photos to the local police station, which she said she would give to them this morning when she went shopping. I had a call half an hour ago from the local police to say the photos are now en-route to us as we speak."

"I should leave you both on your own more often! Great work, well done! I was going to set this research this afternoon, but you've beaten me to it." She took the last mouthful of her chicken pizza, licked her fingers, and had a last mouthful of coffee. "Okay, where's the receipt for these pizzas? I'll reimburse you. My shout for a job well done."

Stan smiled at her. "Thanks, Boss. But it was our job...and the pizzas, well, they were our pleasure, judging by the empty boxes."

Jane said, "Well, thank you again. I'll now quickly update you both on Steve Ho's case, which we discussed before I came here today. Firstly, Pierre has admitted to forging paperwork for Dr Stapleton for use at the Melbourne Central Hospital Morgue and at the funeral Parlour."

"What a little creep!" growled Stan. "So he's going to get a lighter sentence for being a special witness? I hope not!"

"At the moment, Bluey, Ho's squad are letting him tell them information, and also currently not advising one way or the other on any court leniency of course, when their case is wrapped up ready for the court proceedings, Ho will hand him over to the fraud squad."

"Good!" grinned Stan. "It couldn't happen to a nicer shit. He won't get a suspended sentence the second time around, that's for sure."

"Steve also told me that Pierre and Loretta have counter alibis, which I pointed out may not be fool proof, because Pierre could have been stoned on drugs the night his father was murdered. I don't think he killed his father. He hated him, yes, because he believed that his father was responsible for his mother's death."

"Hang on, it took two people to tango to produce a child, so his mother was equal in the production of the stillborn child. His mother and the baby's death was simply a tragedy that happened at the time." grumbled Stan.

"I couldn't have put it more succinctly myself, Bluey," grinned Jane. "Ho's team are now checking Loretta's movements that night. She was prone to going out late at night, as Pierre has admitted in his interview. So my guess is that she's involved in Professor Johann de Jong's murder, along with Dr Stapleton. Stapleton left Melbourne Central under a cloud, too, resigned before he was sacked for twilighting in the hospital morgue with an unconfirmed accomplice. At least, that's the gossip."

Angela added, "It looks like they have two good suspects. I reckon Graham Pappas is becoming our prime suspect, isn't he? Why are you so certain, Boss?"

"Just a gut feeling, that's all. You said that the Brunswick address was his last known address? Where is he now?"

Angela responded, "A good question. That's why I think Stan and I might have to go to his last employer, a building company in Brunswick. He was employed as a carpenter with them. I reckon someone there just might know where he is or what he intended to do when he left them."

"Okay, Angel, you go with Bluey and see what you can find out. If his picture arrives in the meantime, I can always take a photo of one received and send it to your mobile."

"That's great. Come on, Bluey let's clear this lunch stuff before we go." She turned to Jane and added, "I'll phone you if we find out anything."

Stan grinned. "Regular little housewife, aren't you, Angel. Come on, give me the boxes and I'll take them to the bin. You can put the cups into the dishwasher."

Five minutes later, Stan and Angela left the office. Stan waved briefly at Jane, "See you in a couple of hours, Boss."

Detective Sergeant Mary Lamb and Detective Constable Charles Chan joined Sergeant Jason Standing with forensic officers from Jason's Broadmeadows CID office. They had come armed with a search warrant for Dr Stapleton's Funeral Parlour in Fawkner.

Mary whispered to Jason as they searched through paperwork in Stapleton's office, "I just loved the look of surprise and then almost horror on Stapleton's face when you produced your search warrant, love!"

"Yep, had the desired effect, didn't it? I've got one of my officers to keep an eye on him at all times, just to make sure that he doesn't try to hide or destroy anything we might be interested in."

"It's still okay for tonight?"

"Of course! I'll pick you up at seven. Got a table booked at the Crown in the city." He put his head next to her ear, and added very quietly, "And a room booked for the night, as arranged."

Mary giggled, and replied, "I'm taking my extra-large handbag with me. I'm all prepared. Looking forward to tonight," she winked.

Their conversation was interrupted by a forensic officer, whose face had a big grin. "Look at what we've just found in the back shed, Sir." He held out a labelled evidence bag, which contained empty syringes and empty phials labelled Chloral Hydrate and Sodium Thiopental.

"Good work!"

"I think someone forgot to put that bin out for the rubbish collection, fortunately for us. We're also looking around for fingerprints to cross-match with Dr Stapleton, Loretta Stevens and Pierre de Jong...and, of course, with the victim, Johann de Jong. I reckon this could be the murder scene, Sir."

"While you're checking, have a thorough look at the hearse, but more importantly, his private station wagon. Take it in to our garage for testing if necessary, Mike."

"Yes, Sir!" was the reply as he left.

Charlie came into the room. "It's looking good, you two!" He grinned when Jason and Mary both blushed. "I'm talking about the forensics, guys!"

"You're right about the forensics, Charlie, this place is beginning to look like a gold mine. Steve Ho will be delighted by the time we finish here, I reckon."

At three o'clock, Jane was sitting at her desk, looking at copies of photos sent to her office from the Victoria Police at Moonee Ponds. *Tall, slim build, pale skin, blond hair, and muscular. Well, he's in the building industry, after all.* She photographed the best image, and sent copies to both Angela and Stan. She jumped as her mobile buzzed and rang in her hand.

"Bluey? How's it going?"

"Better than expected, Boss. Thanks for the photos. Apparently, our blond haired boy shot a couple of nails through his foot with a nail gun a couple of weeks ago. He was laid off on compo, but hasn't returned yet. He left his rented flat in Brunswick according to his ex-flat mate, one of the builders here. But his mate was asked to re-direct mail for the first month to a post office box in Fitzroy."

"So we can hopefully trace his real address at that post office?"

"Hope so, but now the big news. The first couple of weeks the mail was redirected to addressee Mr. Graham Pappas, then about a week ago, there was a letter addressed and re-directed to a Mr. Graham Polites!"

"He's changed his name?"

"Don't know if is official or forged, Boss...at this moment, anyway. Angel and I are going to the Fitzroy Post Office en route back to you to get this Graham's home address, which should be on the original re-direction paperwork. It looks like he might be living nearby to this Post Office. We've nearly got him, Boss!"

"Again, well done, both of you! I'll see you soon." Jane then sat back in her chair, her thoughts racing. *I hope my gut feeling is right I'm so proud of my squad, just the right people. I like the way they went ahead with enquiries whilst I was occupied. That's what cold cases are all about. Searching different possibilities and going on hunches, and then getting evidence and proof. Normally in such police work, the dead can only reveal what happened to them via forensic evidence, and that's what we need here. Thank goodness my team don't know about my eerie information from the victim. Mind you, I wonder if Angel doesn't know or suspect, after five years of marriage to Steve Ho, there wouldn't be many secrets. If she does know, she's certainly not telling anyone, thank goodness!*

Jane's mobile buzzed and vibrated around her desk, startling her back to reality.

"Steve? What's up?"

"Just had to tell you. Charlie and Bah Bah have found a gold mine of evidence, particularly in the back shed. An old garbage bin contained empty syringes, and empty phials of Chloral Hydrate and Sodium Thiopental. Certainly not stuff that would be used in a funeral parlour on dead people. And more to the point, they are the substances found in Johann de Jong's body! Stapleton's big mistake was tossing them into the bin in the shed, or someone else did. They're bagged as evidence and will be fingerprinted and DNA checked, of course. How often have we, in the past, found incriminating evidence because either the murderer was too confident, careless or simply forgetful in one small detail?"

"Definitely. Well done! Keep in touch, mate. If fingerprints and DNA match Stapleton's and Loretta's, you have your murderers."

"I'm confident that we'll get the matching prints. There are another set of prints in the shed too, on a glass, plus prints on two other glasses, all of which haven't been washed, sitting on a bench. We have taken these glasses as evidence too. Again...carelessness or panic?"

"Hmm, I wonder if the different prints belong to the Professor, Steve."

"Now there's a good thought, Boss! I'm confident about the prints and DNA samples taken from the phials, syringes and boxes, bags, and the glasses. Hopefully, the glasses have traces of whisky in them, confirming that was where the professor was given his *Mickey Finn*. Fingers crossed that we'll bring them to face our charges."

"I'm really pleased for you, mate. It's been a nasty case, but I think you've done it."

"I'll let you know. Speak to you soon, Boss."

Jane smiled as she reflected how, even after several years of not working with Ho, that he still called her Boss. It was a term of endearment as well as respect. A thought suddenly came to her. *Steve keeps saying that he misses working with me. I wonder if he is trying for a change of position. Heck, I'd love him on my squad again, and I reckon he'd work professionally with his wife, Angel. He's been in charge of the special homicide squad for five years, ever since I left to do lecturing, that's a long time. I'd bet he'd appreciate having regular hours too. I know Angel does, and so do I. It would be better for their kids too, to have their mum and dad home at more certain times. Heck, I'd better keep these thoughts on the back burner, until both our cases have been concluded.*

Her phone buzzed around her desk top again. "Angel?"

"Hi Boss, the post office has been most helpful. We have copies of the documentation that a Mr Graham Polites--formerly Pappas--completed to pay the post office to forward his mail to his new address, starting next week to the actual place that he's now living. He still has to give them a copy of his deed poll to show them why his name changed. He apparently applied to change his name to Polites two weeks ago, using his birth certificate to show his mother's name, and he'd apparently shown them a copy of his mother's marriage certificate. I'm not sure how he got a copy of the marriage certificate, though. Maybe he paid for it, or perhaps he stole that from the Polites' home somehow? Time will tell, eh, when we catch this guy."

"So where is he living now?"

"He's renting a small flat in Fitzroy, not far from this post office. We have his home phone number and mobile number too. Well, the numbers that he gave the post office, anyway. He's got an appointment at eleven tomorrow morning to give them a certified copy of his deed poll."

"Okay, in the meantime we need to get a warrant to search his flat, and that will take some time. So you can get the warrant first, and then come back here. I think we'll surprise him tomorrow after his visit to the post office."

"Okay, Boss. Bluey and I are leaving now. We'll go to our favourite magistrate to get a warrant. See you in an hour? Or maybe not," she added as an afterthought, "It's already four and by the time we get the warrant, it will be home time. It's my turn to pick up the kids from my parents."

"No problem, Angel. I'll be leaving at five. I'll see you both at eight thirty tomorrow morning in the office."

"Okay. Looks like a good day coming up. See you in the morning."

For the next hour, Jane sorted out pending paperwork needing signatures and decisions, then closed up the office and went to her car to drive home.

Jane was greeted by her two excited brown and white happy Cavalier King Charles dogs who always beat Oliver out of the door to greet her. He finally emerged from the front door, holding a pair of cooking tongs, and wearing his favourite barbeque apron.

"Hello, my love," Oliver greeted her as she arrived home, "The barbeque is fired up; sausages are ready to pop on, with some hens' eggs, accompanied by baked beans. I felt like surprising you with something casual for a change. The dogs can have a sausage each in their dinner, too."

"Sounds yummy. I'm starving," she lied. *I can't tell him I've pigged out with a large pizza for lunch. So much for a healthy diet today!*

An hour later, after dinner, Jane looked at her watch. "Oh, Oliver, I'd better check out the back to see if my ghost is there wanting to talk to me, as I suggested to her this morning."

"Vicki's ghost knows our place?"

"Yep, she's been here several times, unknown to either of us at the time, apparently!"

"You'd better go then. I'll keep the dogs here in case they spook her." He laughed. "Sorry about that pun, not intended, my love."

Jane walked out the back door onto the verandah. "Vicki?"

"I'm here. I was listening to you inside. I guessed Oliver can't see me. The dogs don't either. I thought they might have sensed that I was hovering around. But they didn't."

"Thanks for being here, Vicki as promised. Have you thought of anything else?"

"No, sorry. But it's nice to talk to someone. It's weird being a ghost. I don't feel hungry, or tired, or hot or cold or wet for that matter. It's, well, just weird... I just want you to find this man, so I can finally have peace. My mum and dad will find peace then too, won't they?"

"Yes, they will, Vicki. I'm going back inside now. It's cold out here for me, even if it isn't for you. I'll see you tomorrow evening, if you like, straight after I come home and before Oliver and I have dinner...how does that sound?"

"That's good. I like talking with you. See you then, Jane Doe."

With those words, Vicki disappeared. Jane returned into the warm house, thinking, *there's times like this when I hate my name. Jane Doe...especially as most of my career has been dealing with dead people, and unidentified bodies in morgues labelled John Doe or Jane Doe. I reckon my late father's policeman's sense of humour contributed to my name!*

Oliver handed her a hot mug of coffee.

"Anything new to report, Jane?"

"Nope. Poor thing just wants company to talk to. It must be a terrible condition to be a ghost! She wants to chat to me again tomorrow as soon as

I get home, which I will do. With luck, I'll have good news for her; and hopefully, and in a way, rather sadly, I won't see her again."

Day Six

Jane drove to work very early the next morning, with some quiet classical music playing on the audio USB stick in her car.

I can feel we're going to break this case today. At last we've found the missing member of the Polites' family, Graham Pappas, I mean Graham Polites. I wonder if he's the same Graham that Loretta mentioned, whom she met with Pierre at a night club. Hang on! If this is the Graham who went to Melbourne Grammar with Pierre, then it would have been so easy for Pierre to forge a marriage certificate for his old school chum to help him change his name. Well, that's something we can ask him when we interview him.

Ho's team sat in his office at eight with big grins. They were all armed with fresh hot large cups of coffee and toasted egg sandwiches bought at the canteen on the ground floor. It was a breakfast conference. Mary was the first to speak. She pulled her warm scarf off from around her neck, her blond, frizzy hair bounced around her shoulders.

"Boss, we've collected two sets of fingerprints in the out shed that don't belong to Dr Stapleton. One set belongs to Loretta Stevens. The other set matches Professor Johann de Jong!"

Charlie added, "Yeah Boss, it looks like you're correct. They obviously had an unexpected visit from the Professor at the funeral parlour. My guess is that Stapleton and Stevens offered their guest a small drink of whisky, being friendly and cordial or whatever. Time will tell when we re-question the two of them."

Ho said, "Yes, the Mickey Finn drug was put into his whisky, which was detected in his autopsy, then once he was drugged to sedation, one of them injected the lethal doses of drugs to kill him." Ho looked at Mary and continued, "Anything else, Bah Bah?"

"Yes, we also found a tarpaulin in the back of Stapleton's station wagon. It's currently at the forensic lab being examined for De Jong's DNA, as is the car itself. The car has some dirt and grass on the tyres, which we hope match the unmade track that runs along the end of Patullos Lane to the railway line."

Charlie Chan fiddled with his pitch black ponytail and flicked it out from under his warm sweater. His black eyes glistened in the early morning light coming in through the office windows. "Boss, I've checked with Sergeant Jason Standing, who confirmed that the gate leading to this track was unlocked. In fact, the lock was broken...according to the Melbourne Water Board, who maintains the park area and interlocking lakes in the area. I reckon that's how Stapleton and Stevens got through the gate and were able to take de Jong's body out of the back of the station wagon in the dark of the night, quietly take it out of the tarpaulin, and dump it into the lake." Chan smiled and took another mouthful of his toasted sandwich. "Mmm, this is a perfect breakfast for a bachelor!"

Mary Lamb's mobile rang. "Hi Jason. Yes, we're here with Detective Inspector Steve Ho. He's now up to date with what we found at Stapleton's

Funeral parlour." She giggled and then blushed, "Hum, err...yes, I'll see you after work." Her cheeks got redder as Ho and Chan both grinned at her.

Ho said, "Hmmm, am I detecting a little romance blossoming between you two?"

Mary sighed, "Oh, okay, yes we've become an item, if you like. He's a really nice guy."

Ho smiled at her again, "Sorry, I'm not prying, just pleased for you both. I reckon you're well matched, actually." He winked at Charlie.

Jane entered the empty office and sat at her desk, checking all the paperwork that had seemed to magically appear since she last looked now piled up in her in-tray. *Hell, I hate the paperwork side of this job. Don't be silly, Jane, it's often paperwork that can be used as hard evidence in court.*

Half an hour later, she poured some hot water into a mug in the kitchenette, made a coffee for herself, and went to the conference room, where she had put a pile of papers, and sat down. *Heck, it's quiet in here.*

Stan's booming voice broke the silence.

"Top of the morning, Boss."

Angela's dulcet tones followed.

"Morning, Boss, it's going to be a great day. I can feel it!"

The door opened again. Dr Fred Harvey entered, nodded at Jane, and then gave her a wink.

"Have you heard the news, Jane?"

"What news?"

"My friends at the central forensic labs have told me that the evidence that Ho's team collected yesterday from Stapleton's funeral home have matching fingerprints of Dr Henry Stapleton *and* Loretta Stevens on the phials and syringes!"

Jane's hazel eyes were now wide and she replied, "Hey, that's terrific news!"

Fred had a sip of his coffee before continuing his news. "The forensic team have also found some other incriminating paperwork in that bin, which also has their fingerprints. Plus they collected prints from the three glasses that were found on the work bench. Two of the glasses contained remnants of whisky and also have their fingerprints. The third glass also contained whisky and dregs of Chloral Hydrate. They were checking the finger prints on that glass when I left the office last night."

Jane put her thumb in the air, "I bet you anything that Professor de Jong's prints are on that glass, mate! Steve and his team will be pretty chuffed. They can finally pin murder charges on Stapleton and Stevens. What a pair...not only murderers, but also involved in illegal transplant tissue smuggling. Hope the courts throw the book at them." She paused a moment, her hand twiddling her auburn ponytail. "I guess Pierre will be a prosecution witness in the case, and will also be charged with forgery of the documents."

Fred nodded, "That's the plan, I believe. At least he didn't kill his father. Silly bugger was completely fooled by Loretta's charms, and in doing so, was an accessory to her getting illegal papers signed for transplant ops with tissues on burn victims and goodness knows what other sort of ops." He shrugged his shoulders. "Time will tell, of course."

"Fred, have you caught up with Bluey and Angel's success yesterday?"

"I've heard rumours...just kidding...yes, we three have just shared a quick coffee downstairs."

Jane laughed. "I should have guessed. Well everyone, let's set up our plans for today to catch and then have a formal chat with our Graham Polites."

She went to the electronic board on the wall, and pointed to an enlarged copy of a google map which she had found, showing the area in Fitzroy where the post office was situated. "Graham is due to visit the post office at ten forty-five. We'll get there before then, park nearby, and watch. Once he's spotted, we'll wait until he's given in his deed poll copy, then follow him at a discreet distance back to his flat, which is only a couple of blocks away from the post office." She pointed to another section on the map. "I'm led to believe that he doesn't have a car. So he'll be on foot. Once he gets home, we'll go in with our warrant."

"Nice surprise for the lad, Boss," said Stan.

"That's the intention, Stan. Okay, we leave in half an hour."

At ten o'clock, Jane, Stan and Angela drove to Fitzroy. Twenty minutes later, they parked at a discrete distance from the post office, where they could still observe who entered and left the building. At ten thirty, the figure of Graham Polites limped into the post office, holding an envelope.

Jane said, "Right, I'll go into the post office. The staff haven't met me, so I can hover around the racks of envelopes and cards and eavesdrop on what he's doing. Then I can casually follow him out and join you. We can follow him at a safe distance to his flat, armed with our warrant!"

It was nearly ten minutes later before Jane returned to the unmarked police car. She shut the door. "I came out first. He's about to leave. There was a long queue this morning of mainly pensioners paying bills. Yesterday was pension day. He was getting very agitated. He even started to ask one of the staff if they could open another position at the counter to speed things up!"

"Impatient young man. Bet you he thinks that he's got away with murder?" remarked Stan. "Could be right, mate. I agree that at the moment, he's our prime suspect."

Jane pointed to the entrance. "There he is!"

The tall, blond-haired figure hobbled up the street.

Angel said, "Looks like he really messed up his foot."

Stan replied, "Doesn't it. His ex-flat mate said that there was severe nerve damage done by the nail-gun. Apparently three nails went into his foot. The silly idiot forgot to take his finger off the trigger after the first shot!"

Jane added, "Could be poetic justice, I reckon. Okay, let's follow him once he's turned the first corner. Then park again for a few minutes. He's pretty slow."

It took Graham Polites nearly ten minutes to shuffle down the street and finally turn the corner. Stan started the car and drove slowly to the corner, turned and parked.

Stan said, "There's his flat down there on the right, Boss. I'll wait until he goes inside before we drive down there."

"Good idea, mate," replied Jane.

Graham Polites finally entered the ground floor unit. As soon as the door shut, Stan restarted the car and drove down opposite the units. The three Special Cold Case Squad members got out and walked over to the unit.

Jane turned to Stan, and said in a low voice, "Stan, could you check around the back?"

"I don't think I'll need to, Boss. He's too slow to run."

"You're not wrong there," she replied. Jane rang the bell, thinking. *Come on! Come on! Answer your door!*

The door finally opened. Graham's bright blue eyes bulged when he saw three people at his door.

"Yes? What do you want?" he asked.

Jane showed her ID, in unison with Angela and Stan. "I'm Detective Chief Superintendent Doe, this is Detective Sergeant Johnson, and this is Detective Constable Nguyen..."

"You must have the wrong place and person; I've done nothing wrong!" Beads of sweat started to appear on his upper lip.

Jane continued, "Graham Polites, formerly Pappas, we have a search warrant to inspect your premises."

With those words, Stan's burley figure quietly pushed Graham back inside and against the hall wall, as he said firmly, "Time to let us in, mate."

They all entered and followed Graham into the small lounge room on the right.

Stan commanded, "Sit down Graham, and listen to what we have to say."

Jane sat down, and Stan sat next to the lounge room door. There was nowhere for Graham Polites to go. Angela quietly disappeared down the hallway by herself.

Jane said, "We work for the Special Cold Case Squad. We're re-investigating the death of one Vicki Polites, whom you know as your half-sister."

Graham shrank back into his chair, hands clasped tightly on his lap.

"Vicki? Her death was...was an accident." His Adam's apple started to bob up and down as he kept swallowing.

Jane continued, "Graham, we need a DNA sample from you, plus your fingerprints."

"Oh, so you want to eliminate me from your enquiries?" His eyes darted about nervously.

Stan ignored the last comment, and produced the DNA and fingerprint equipment from the satchel that Angela had brought in. He put on his forensic gloves, picked a swab out of a special phial, and said, "This won't take a minute, Graham. Open your mouth please." He swabbed Graham's mouth, and then put the swab back into the pre-labelled phial. "Now give me your right hand," he took the finger prints one by one. "Now the left hand, please." Graham had now turned a pasty colour, with beads of sweat showing on his forehead, whilst Stan completed his tasks. Finally Stan said, "Thanks for your cooperation. It's appreciated."

Jane had watched in silence as Stan gathered the DNA and fingerprints, and put them into evidence bags, her mind racing with thoughts.

By the end of today, after we've interviewed you, we should have the concrete evidence of your presence in Vicki's bedroom, plus matched your DNA on Vicki's pyjamas! You won't be able to refute that in court, mate!

Angela appeared at the lounge room door. She said, quietly, "Boss, can I see you for a moment?"

"Of course."

They both moved outside the lounge room and went down the hall. Stan positioned himself in front of Graham, and said, "Stay exactly where you are, mate."

Angela said, "Follow me, Boss. We've hit a goldmine of stuff." She guided Jane to Graham's small bathroom. "Look, newspaper clippings in this box. They're all about the Polites. Looks like he's been a bit obsessive about the family. Plus I've found the Polites Marriage Certificate over here." She led Jane to his bedroom, and pointed to a small desk against the wall. "I reckon it was forged."

"Angel, we'll ask him about this when we question him at the station."

"So you're going to charge him?"

Jane was also looking through the papers on the desk. She looked up at Angela and replied, "Oh, yes! Ah good girl, you also found the paperwork for the deed poll for his name change. I agree the marriage certificate could be forged, most likely by Pierre. I reckon Graham and Pierre both went to school together at Melbourne Grammar, just like the lovely Loretta told us."

"Here's the piece de resistance, Boss." Angela handed Jane a diary.

"Well done. Hell, it's full of notes about finding out about his adoption." Jane flicked through the pages, and read some of the contents. *'Why did she dump me? Spoilt little Vicki. I want what she has. I want that painting.'* Oh my God! Did you read this?" asked Jane.

"Yes, parts of it. It's disturbing stuff. It makes my skin crawl to read it." Mary held up her right hand at Jane. "Now, it's time for a quick high five, Boss." The two women smacked their hands together. "We've got him!"

"Yes, we have. The DNA swabs should confirm that he was in the room with Vicki the night she died. Okay, let's go back and advise Graham Polites of his rights, and then charge him and take him back to the station for questioning."

Graham glowered at Jane when she entered the lounge room. Half an hour later, Graham Polites, in handcuffs, was escorted out of his unit by Stan Johnson. Jane and Angela carefully carried out the evidence bags containing the DNA, fingerprints and all the paperwork from the bathroom and bedroom.

The special Cold Case Squad then drove their prisoner to the St. Kilda Road complex.

Forty minutes later, Jane and Stan sat opposite Graham Polites. They had deliberately made him sit on his own in the interview room whilst they observed him through the one-way window.

After the introductory formalities, with the digital recorder turned on, Jane started to put items on the table in front of him; paper clippings about his family, the copy of his deed poll, the copy of the Polites marriage certificate, and finally, Graham's diary that Angela had found in his bedside table.

"So, you've been a busy lad since you first met your biological mother and half-sister, haven't you?" Jane asked.

Graham pouted his lips, frowned, and replied, "Just getting my life into order, that's all."

Jane thought, *defiant little sod!* She responded, "So you got your ex-school buddy to forge a copy of his parent's marriage certificate?"

Graham brushed his right hand through his unruly blond hair, then said, "I... I um...ah... Yes! Why not? She dumped me, the bitch. I've only recently found out that I was adopted. My parents, or I should say, my adoptive parents, are all fair haired, so I blended in. However, all those years I've lived with them, I never, ever felt like I belonged. They were all such goody goodies. They kept telling me I had a temper. Must have been from my biological father, whoever he is. Shit, how do I know?" Graham shifted himself forward on his seat, hands folded tightly on the table in front of him. "As for that precious little Vicki...spoilt little brat, I reckon!" He suddenly stopped talking. His head dropped onto his chest, lips pouting again. After a few minutes silence, he looked up at Jane and Stan and added, "Shit, I'm in trouble, aren't I?"

Stan pointed to the newspaper clippings of MP John Polites. "So why collect all this information about your step father?" He then pointed to the marriage certificate copy, and the deed poll copy. "Let's face it, mate, you didn't have to get this paperwork illegally. But of course, you knew your school chum was a great forger, didn't you. Obviously he owed you something, and he did it for free for you, huh?"

"Nope, I paid Pierre. He needed the money for drugs. He's an addict. Used to be cocaine, now he's into ice. Silly bugger!"

"So Pierre de Jong went to school with you. It was very convenient, for you that he could forge papers, wasn't it?" Stan suddenly slapped his hand down on the table. "And how, for God's sake can you explain the pure evil written in your diary?"

Graham simply shrugged his shoulders, "Dunno, really."

Stan retorted, "Yes, you're in heaps of trouble, mate. In fact, you're up to your neck in it. We've already advised you of your rights twice today; once at your flat, and again before we started this interview. But you refused to have a solicitor present. Do you wish to have one now?"

"Hell no!" he slammed his fist on the table, then thumped himself on his chest, and shouted, "I can look after myself!"

Jane spoke next, in a very quiet, soft voice. "Graham, by what we've been reading in your diary, you wanted what Vicki had for yourself?"

Graham scowled at Jane. "Yes! I wanted that painting. It's valuable, you know, I've checked."

Jane continued, "So you sneaked into the Polites house that fateful night, after you'd drugged the nearly empty bottle of wine downstairs to make the babysitter sleep. Am I right, so far?"

Graham nodded, and a slight smile appeared on his face. *What a creep!* Jane added, "Good. Then you crept upstairs to Vicki's room. But she woke, didn't she? So what happened next, Graham? In your own words. Take your time."

"I was about to take the painting off the wall when she woke up. I put my hand over her mouth and whispered to her to keep quiet. Her eyes were popping, she was scared...that's what I wanted. She was clutching her stupid teddy. I whispered to her that I'd take his head off if she uttered a sound!"

Jane could feel goose bumps on her arms and on the back of her neck. *Purely evil, but not insane...no, you're the spoilt self-centred brat, not Vicki!* "And of course, Vicki kept quiet, didn't she?"

"Yes. But as I went to get the painting again she tossed the teddy across the room, and tried to get out of the bed and run away, but I grabbed her. She struggled, I put my hand over her mouth, and she bit my finger. The bitch! I... I... I... lost it. She tried to kick me. We were both out on the landing at that stage and she wriggled free for a second, I grabbed her again, and then I pushed her down the stairs."

Stan said, "Her scream woke up the babysitter, didn't it?"

Graham pulled out a handkerchief and wiped his sweaty face, "Yeah! That's when I had to leave the painting behind, damn it, and I went down the stairs and out the front door."

Stan's voice was now loud as he spoke; his grey-flecked ginger hair glowed in the overhead light. "You left your half-sister, who shared the same blood as you, helpless on the floor at the bottom of the stairs?"

Graham's eyes were now wide open, his face going red as he replied, "I had to get out. The bloody babysitter would have got a description of me in the well-lit hallway. What could I have done? I'm not a doctor, for Christ's sake!"

Stan shook his head. "Compassionate little sod, aren't you. She was your half-sister, and you left her to die. You could have called Triple Zero at the very least!"

Graham was suddenly quiet, and started to bight his lower lip. "Oh shit! Shit! Shit!"

Stan asked, "So you'd drugged the wine that the babysitter drank?"

"Yeah! I'd put a few sleeping pills into the wine bottle that had been left for Loretta, in the kitchen, before I went upstairs."

Stan smiled at Graham. "Ah, so you know Loretta?"

"Yeah, of course I do. We met her at a night club a while back. She shacks up with Pierre sometimes. I know about the forging that he does for her...that's why I left before she saw me. Don't you understand?"

Jane then spoke, "So you asked Pierre to forge the marriage and the deed poll certificates, so you could have your name changed to Polites? Otherwise, you threatened Pierre that you'd tell the police about his forging activities. Nice friend, aren't you?"

"So what? Yeah, my plan was to ingratiate myself into the Polites family fold, so to speak, I wanted an MP to be my step-father. He has loads of money, too. But in the meantime, Pierre's father was murdered! Pierre was worried that he could be in trouble with the police because they would find out about his forgery work for Dr Stapleton and Loretta..." Graham went silent for a moment again, and then added "Shit, I'm in a real mess now!" He dropped his head and sat in silence as Jane spoke.

"Graham Polites, as you're charged with the murder of Vicki Polites, you will be taken to the Central Remand Centre to be held until the Magistrates Court hears the charges against you. Depending upon whether you plead guilty or not guilty, your case may go to trial at a later date. That, mate, is entirely up to you. I still suggest you get a solicitor."

Graham pouted again. "Hell, I'm bloody guilt...what's the point of spending money on a solicitor." Again, he went silent.

Stan called in the uniformed police who were waiting outside the interview room. They came in, re-cuffed Graham Polites, then took him away to the lift, that took them to the Police wagon in the underground car park, in which they would then drive him to the Central Remand Centre.

Jane high fived Stan and grinned. "With a bit of luck, the Magistrate will see him tomorrow and keep him in custody for a committal hearing. We've got the bastard, mate!"

Angela Nguyen and Dr Fred Harvey had watched the interview in the adjacent room. Angela rushed up and hugged both Stan and Jane. Fred gave Stan a big firm handshake, Jane an elegant kiss on the back of her hand, and said, "Great interview, you two! I've got all the forensics labelled and stored away, ready for the committal hearing. He'll plead guilty. I don't think he wants the publicity, but he's going to get it anyway, via the popularity of his step-father. I reckon his twisted personality and temper came from his biological father. I wonder what happened to him."

Jane said, "From what Janet told me, he disappeared off the landscape as soon as he knew that she was pregnant!"

Stan looked at his watch. "It's time for lunch, Boss."

"Good idea, Bluey..." Jane's phone buzzed in her trouser pocket. "Steve?" she said as she answered, "Yes, why not. I'll see you downstairs. We can chat over some quick lunch, if you like."

"Having lunch with my husband?" asked Angela. "Tell him I'm having lunch with two lovely men up here," she said, pointing to Stan and Fred.

Everyone laughed.

Steve met Jane outside the café.

"I thought you lot would be celebrating with a drink!"

"Later, mate. There's still a lot of paperwork to be done and we're hoping for the backup of positive DNA tests that we took from Graham Polites this morning. They should back up the fact that he was present in Vicki's room, and that he had held her against her will, then murdered her in a fit of rage and jealousy."

They sat down and ordered some toasted sandwiches and coffee.

"Jane, he might try for insanity."

"He refuses to use a solicitor. If he did plead insanity or temporary insanity, it won't work. He simply has a bad temper. The Pappas family will confirm this, according to what he revealed to us in his interview. That's it!"

"Well done, Boss." Ho winked at her.

"Steve, what's the latest on Stapleton and Loretta?"

"When you were interviewing Polites, we were interviewing Stapleton. He's fessed up to the fact that Loretta and he had drugged, and then killed Professor Johann de Jong. They wrapped him in a tarpaulin, then took him to Bridgewater Lake and dumped him in. Like your case, we also have forensic backup with fingerprints and DNA in the shed, the station wagon and on the tarpaulin to prove this was so." Ho started his toasted cheese and tomato sandwich. "Hmm, just what I needed. Oh, Stapleton told us that Pierre de Jong had accidentally let some copying cum forging work behind in his father's office, which we've also now got as evidence. You might like to have a loan of it for your case. He was practising his mother's and father's signatures."

"Ah, the signatures and certificates he needed for Graham Polites!"

"Exactly! Professor de Jong had found them in his office bin one night. He'd gone to Stapleton's office to confront him with being involved with the illegal documentation of transplant organs in Australia. Loretta was there, with Stapleton, so they were both in danger from Johann de Jong. They offered him a small drink and said they'd like to talk about his accusations. That's when they slipped the micky finn drug into his whisky. Once he was unable to move or resist, they injected an overdose of drugs to kill him. The rest you know. Stapleton said that he just had to keep de Jong quiet. He even tried to justify his clandestine work, telling us that he'd helped dozens of people live...so in his eyes, it was justified! One big point was that he couldn't explain why they'd killed such a brilliance surgeon. Bit of a creep, in my humble opinion."

Jane swallowed the last of her toasted chicken sandwich and said, "Creep...that's the same word I used to describe Graham Polites. I'd rather remember him as Graham Pappas...but that would also insult the Pappas family."

"Stapleton told us that Loretta only shacked up with Pierre de Jong because of his forging skills, and that she was actually his mistress, not Pierre's. He essentially tried to suggest that Loretta had nagged him into the murder that night when she knew that de Jong was coming to the funeral home. That's some weird loyalty for you. They both deserve each other!"

"So your case is basically closed too! Well done, Steve."

Ho smiled at her and said, "It's been a pleasure working with you again, Boss." He looked at his watch. "I'd better go and do some paperwork so Angel and I can get home at a reasonable time together, for a change."

"Before you go, Steve, I've a question to ask you," Jane said, "You shouldn't answer straight away, but discuss with Angel at home tonight."

"Okay, you've now wetted my curiosity, Jane Doe...go ahead and ask the question."

"Before I ask the question, I'll let you know that the Assistant Commissioner has actually said yes to my suggestion. I spoke to him about this earlier today on the phone."

"Go on, Jane...I'm fascinated."

"Well, you have a great team working for you in the Special Crime Squad, which you've certainly handled brilliantly since I left five years ago, to go away from the pointy end, as we say, and do my MBA part time, whilst lecturing at the Police Academy. Sorry, I'm digressing, but I want to praise your work like the Assistant Commissioner has. When I set up the Special Cold Case Squad, I actually chose Angel ahead of you because I knew she needed the regular hours so she could manage my two beautiful God-children."

Steve nodded at her to continue.

"That said, the Assistant Commissioner and I also both could see that you should be promoted, sometime to Detective Chief Inspector Ho. But at the moment, this isn't possible in the Special Crime Squad because of budget constraints. However, a Sergeant Jason Standing of Broadmeadows, CID, requested last year if he could apply for a position in the city in plain clothes work. His work is outstanding, as you have said. He'd make a great replacement for you..."

Steve Ho smiled, "One member of my team would be over the moon about that... Bah Bah. They've been seeing each other the last week. I believe they are becoming...let's say, *attached* to each other. The AC may not like that! Both in the one team..."

"Funnily enough, quite the contrary. He likes the idea of you moving up and across to my team, even though your wife is already in the squad. Bit of a forward-thinking guy, our new AC."

Ho's eyes glistened. "Boss, this would be terrific! I am getting a bit stale in my current position. I guess, because I've been working closely with you again. It's sort of emphasised the fact that we work so well together. I miss Fred Harvey too! Hmm, okay, I'll have a long chat with Angel tonight. I need to see how she feels about this first. Please don't tell her at the moment. Bloody Hell, it would be nice to have some so-called normal office hours after fifteen years of shifts and having to be called on at all hours in Homicide and the Special Crime Squad."

Ho got up. "Permission to give you a hug, Boss?"

"Granted!"

Back in the office, Angela had organised a 'pretend' champagne toast for finishing the case. She had poured mineral water into paper cups, and opened a bag of potato chips.

"Hello, Boss. I couldn't resist; I just had to have a toast to the first and successful Cold Case of our newly formed squad. The fact that we can't drink and drive home means it's mineral water." She gave a cup to Jane, Stan and Fred, then lifted her cup and said, "Cheers everyone!"

"A great idea, Angel! Thanks for the kind thought." Jane grinned, "While we are gathered together here, I'd like to add another toast to a girl who has given us, unwittingly, so much information to guide me in this case."

"Who are you talking about, Boss?"

"I'm actually talking about the recipient transplant patient who received Vicki Polites heart."

"You've met the recipient?" asked Fred.

"Yes...but unofficially. The recipient is one of Oliver's patients. She was sent to Oliver because after receiving her new heart, she was having nightmares about being killed and thrown down stairs. She was describing a house that she'd never lived in. She described Vicki Polites' house! Oliver was amazed, and so was I. I won't go into any details, as it would compromise her recovery. It would also compromise patient confidentiality. There have been studies on transplant recipients experiencing or knowing things that they've never experienced before...especially heart recipients."

Fred said, "Yes, I've read about that in my paranormal studies on near death experiences. In fact, I collaborated with in Oliver's studies on a similar topic. It's strange, but true. So this girl was getting information from the donated heart? Amazing!"

Angel then spoke, "Aha, that's why you were so convinced that Vicki had been murdered. What a coincidence that the recipient needed a psychologist, and that person was Oliver... Wow!"

"Now, folks, having told you that information, it stays with us, in-house. We can't possibly use this in our reports as facts, because the courts could have a field day! I just wanted to give a toast to this person for having to get through such a terrible time, but being able to let the donor's heart have its say. Heck, saying that sounds a bit weird doesn't it!"

Fred raised his cup, "Here's to a very brave girl's new heart...may it find peace!"

Angel added, "I have a great name for this case, Boss."

"Oh? What would that be?"

"Well, instead of simply labelling it Vicki Polites' cold case, we could add an extra note below; *Haunted Heart*. What do you think?"

Jane's heart felt like it missed a beat. *Heck, Angel knows. I don't think Steve has told her anything, she's just a very cluey person. Haunted Heart – that's what I said to Oliver, the night we talked about Jenny Summers case.* She felt a shiver go down her spine.

"Are you okay, Jane?" asked Fred. "You look like you've seen a ghost," he chuckled.

"Not at all. Just a bit spooky talking about it, that's all. Now come on everyone, let's get the paperwork finalised ready for the Magistrates Court."

Fred held up his hand and added, "Oh, sorry, I nearly forgot, while we were having lunch, I got a call from the forensic labs, the fingerprints we gleaned in Vicki's room, plus the DNA you got, both match the samples taken this morning from Graham Polites!"

Jane responded, "Well, here's another last toast to that evidence. Well done, Fred; and well done, team." Everyone lifted their cups one more time and drank.

Jane then went into her office and sat at her desk.

Hell, that was close... I wonder what made me tell the squad about a literally Haunted Heart?

Three hours later, Jane's Special Cold Case team had left Jane alone, to wend their different ways home.

Jane made a quick phone call to Janet Polites to tell her that she was going to call in and see them both on her way home, to update them on the latest news. She then called Oliver and told him that she might be a little late getting home, and why.

Half an hour later, Jane smiled as she pulled up in the front of the Polites' home. *It's nice to visit people with some good news for a change. I'm beginning to like this new work even more than before!*

Janet opened the door in less than fifteen seconds. *Obviously she's been watching out for my arrival.*

"Hello Jane, please come in. John's home too. We're looking forward to your news."

Janet ushered her into the lounge room. John Polites held out his hand in greeting to Jane.

"Nice to see you so soon, Jane. I suspect that you've got some good news for us? Please take a seat."

"Thanks for your warm welcome. Yes, I come with good news for you. We have been able to arrest and charge someone for the murder of your daughter, Vicki, today."

John exclaimed, "Thank you! That's fast work! Well done. Sorry, I interrupted you; please tell us all about your case."

"Our enquiries led us eventually to one person; one who had originally disappeared, so it was a bit difficult to find him, as he'd had left his last address, and wasn't going to his workplace. But we eventually traced him via his workmate and ex-flat mate. We also had some good co-operation from his new local post office, where his mail was being forwarded by his ex-flat mate."

Janet leaned forward in her chair. "Was it someone we know?"

"I'm afraid so. This is the sad part of my report to you. The person was Graham Pappas, who has, last week, changed his name by deed poll to Polites."

The couple in front of Jane gasped in unison.

Before they could speak, Jane continued. "I actually think that the paperwork used for this name change was forged. That's being checked forensically as we speak. Once verified, that will come up in court. So I think, eventually, Graham will be sentenced under his former surname, Pappas. However, Graham has admitted to killing Vicki in anger in his interview. He's now in the City Remand Centre, awaiting notification of the time the Magistrates Court will see him to charge him. At this stage, they will set a date for sentencing, as I think he'll plead guilty, like he has in his interview and signed statement."

"What a prick!" exclaimed John. He looked at his wife, and then gave her a hug. "I'm sorry love, I know he's your long-lost child...but...but...how could he do such an evil thing to his half-sister?"

Janet looked at her husband and said softly and calmly, "John, let's face it. I never knew Graham as my son. I'm now glad that I didn't get to know him better after that one and only meeting. His father raped me when I was under-age, then disappeared. A few years ago, his mother told me that he'd died of an overdose. All I can say is that he's a chip off his late biological father's block! I can only hate him, and I hope the court throws the book at him."

John kissed his wife's cheek lightly. "Oh, Janet, why didn't you tell me that about Graham's father? If I'd known, I wouldn't have let the bastard into this house in the first place..."

Janet put up her hand. "That's why I didn't tell you. But that's all in the past. It wasn't my fault that he made me pregnant; and the Church, well, now you fully understand why I'm not religious anymore. They took my child from me." She looked at Jane and added, "Thank you so much, Jane, for coming here. We appreciate all that you've done, we really do. I can't say that I really understand my son's hatred and revenge upon me and especially my daughter, but it's all over now, and Vicki can finally rest in peace, and we can both move on." She smiled and nudged John. "Go on, tell Jane our news."

"Janet is two months pregnant. We don't care if it's a boy or girl. He or she will be most welcome and loved, that's for sure," he said.

Jane got up and gave each of the Polites a hug. "Well done, you two, I'm thrilled for you both! Janet, can I ask you for a favour?"

"Of course, anything!"

"Would you please let me take Vicki's teddy, Harry, with me, so I can give him to Vicki's heart recipient?"

Janet's eyes were wide as she replied, "you know who it is?"

"Yes I do, but ethically, I can't tell you. She's a lovely girl, same age as Vicki. I think she'll love to know that Harry can sit next to her favourite teddy called Pooh Bear, on her desk in her bedroom. Vicki's soul, would, in this girl's new heart, also be delighted to have the two bears together. What do you think?"

"Oh yes, what a lovely idea. Our new child will of course have a brand-new teddy. I find that even now, I get upset when I see Harry. So I'm sure he'll be happy to be with Vicki again...well, you know what I mean. Shall we get him now? I know you want to get home yourself."

"Of course. Thanks for doing this, Janet." Jane followed her upstairs. Janet picked up Harry, gave him a big kiss, and then handed him to Jane, "Take care of Vicki for me, Harry."

"I just know he will, Janet."

They went back down stairs.

John ushered Jane to the front door. "Thank you so much for your help, Jane." John said as Jane stood at the front door, about to leave, "We can now both move on, as Janet has said. I know that finally Vicki will be at peace." With those words, he winked at his wife, and then gave Jane a big hug. "Now you'd better get home to your husband."

Jane finally arrived home an hour later. She clutched Harry in her arms as she entered the house; Oliver greeted her and then went back into the kitchen. Sassy and Spunky kept looking at Harry, and tried to sniff him. Jane immediately put Harry up on top of the dining room sideboard out of their reach.

"Sorry you two, but Harry's not yours. He's a present for a special girl."

Oliver called out from the kitchen. "The case is solved?"

Jane took off her coat and joined him. Oliver put the lid back on the crock pot on the bench. "That's tonight's dinner, my love...chicken casserole."

"Not one of our hens?"

"Of course not. I intend that our hens will all live a long life and retirement at *Wyndales*, as we will too, eventually."

Jane and Oliver sat down in the lounge.

"Oliver, in answer to your first question, yes - the case is now solved. We finally caught up with Graham Polites. There was plenty of evidence at his house. He confessed eventually during his interview. His diary that we found was pretty damning...he held heaps of resentment towards his mother, and more particularly towards his half-sister, Vicki. It's proven to be a sad reminder really...the cruelty of the old days, when newborn illegitimate babies were taken from their underage mothers at birth."

"Yep, I've counselled a few people with that background. Will he try to go for mental impairment at the time of Vicki's murder?"

"I don't think so. He's currently feeling very guilty. That's the way I want him to feel. After all, he had been given the privilege of a private school education and a good upbringing by the Pappas family." Jane sighed. "I guess it all went wrong when they finally decided to tell him that he'd been adopted."

"Well, it's all over now, my love. And it's a celebration of sorts. Your first cold case by your great new squad. Well done! I'll open a bottle of champagne to have with our dinner."

"Lovely," Jane smiled, "But, um...I've got one thing to attend to first..."

"Vicki?"

"Yes. I'll only be a short time. By then I'll be listening for the pop of the cork."

Jane picked up Harry and took him with her to the back verandah. Vicki's image immediately appeared before her.

"Harry!"

"Would you like to cuddle him?"

"I can't, silly," and Vicki's ghost chuckled as she put out her hand to touch Harry. "See, my hand went through him. I found out a while ago that I can go through anything; walls, brick fences..."

Jane laughed, and said, "Well, I think Harry will be very happy tomorrow to meet Pooh Bear and, Jenny."

"I'll be there too, Jane, as you know, but..."

"But..." Jane prodded.

"I'll be happy too, but I'm beginning to feel different somehow; like I'm now calm, and not angry anymore. I know you found my murderer. It was Graham, my half-brother... I don't know why he could be so angry and jealous with me. He didn't really know me, after all. But I can't feel sorry for him. When are you going to Jenny's place?"

"Tomorrow morning, first thing. I know you'll be there, because that's where your soul is, inside Jenny's new heart...your old heart."

"I...I'll always be in her heart and soul, Jane. I understand that, now I know that I'm not real anymore. But my heart will live on in Jenny. I like that idea very much..."

"Vicki?"

"Yes, what is it? You look funny...err... surprised or something...you're looking at me in a weird way..."

"Vicki," Jane smiled, "You're fading. You're finally going to find peace at last. Your parents told me this afternoon that they can now start to move on...but they will never forget you."

"I know that; I was there, Jane. I've been following you everywhere, when you have been working." Vicki suddenly grinned, "And I also know that mum is pregnant... Isn't that terrific? They'll have a new child to love!"

"I'm glad you're happy for your parents."

"Jane, I'll be with you tomorrow when you give Harry to Vicki. I guess she doesn't know about me."

Jane shook her head, "No, she doesn't. Ethically, neither Jenny nor her parents will know your name, because by law, dead donors' names are not revealed. I can't even tell her parents your name, let alone tell them that I've been communicating with your ghost!"

"I used to read books which had ghosts in them, so I know what you mean. It's weird being a ghost. But I'm glad I was one for a short time, so I could finally tell my story via Jenny's dreams. I...I didn't mean to give her nightmares."

"I'm sure Jenny's nightmares will stop now, Vicki. She'll never know that it was your ghost that helped me know about your murder. Oliver, as you already guessed, knows about me being able to communicate with ghosts, so that's why we worked together with Jenny during that morning chat...and that's when I was first able to communicate with you."

"So you knew it was me, inside Vicki?"

"Yes!"

"It must be cool being able to talk to the ghosts of your murder victims...bet your squad doesn't know, eh?"

"No, they don't...and never will. I use my ghost chats to help me find the right way to get evidence to convict murderers, if I can. My Cold Case Squad was able to get all the physical evidence to prove that Graham was in your room that night, and had touched you and your pyjamas that night."

There was a loud *POP* from the kitchen, followed by Oliver's voice calling out, "Champagne is being poured, my love."

"I'm coming, Oliver." Jane turned to Vicki, "It's been nice knowing you, Vicki Polites. I just know that you'll be at peace now, and that the special gift of your heart to Jenny will give her a long and happy life too. I'll give an extra special hug to Harry on your behalf tomorrow morning, before I take him inside to give to Jenny."

Vicki's ghostly image flickered and started to fade until Jane could barely see her in the evening light. She whispered, "I love you, Jane Doe," and smiled in thanks before she finally disappeared.

Day Seven

Jane woke feeling refreshed after a good sleep. After she showered and dressed, she went out to the back verandah.

I wonder if Vicki will appear to me again. I really hope she doesn't. Poor thing... going through all that experience after her death.

Oliver's voice snapped her back to reality. "Coffee's ready, my love."

"Oh good. I'm coming in. It's quite chilly out here today."

She went into the warm kitchen. The dogs had just been given their morning food and were licking their chests contentedly.

"Another busy day for you? I suppose the DPP will be taking over the files from you today, ready for the Magistrates hearing. Have they set a time for that yet?"

"I'm afraid not, but I'm hoping, that the Magistrates will hear his charges this afternoon. I'm also crossing my fingers that he'll plead guilty. It'll save the courts a lot of time and money too, if he does, because he will then be remanded to be in custody until the sentencing at a later date."

"Yep! A bit of time in prison on remand will make the little sod realise what a horrendous thing he's done, not only to himself, but to Vicki's family."

Jane had her cereal and orange juice, and then went to gather her satchel and papers. She returned to the kitchen, gave Oliver a kiss, patted the dogs, and said, "I'll see you later. I'm going to work via the Summer's home, to deliver Harry to Jenny."

"I think that gesture is brilliant, I really do. I also like the offer that you've given to Steve. You two make a great team. The fact that Steve also knows about your ethereal powers will help, too." He paused, and added, "You know, I thought last night that maybe Angela might suspect your ghostly abilities."

"Oh Oliver, what made you think that?"

"Just a hunch, that's all...and don't worry your lovely head about that; if she does eventually confide in you, like Steve and myself, she'll keep it private...she's a totally reliable woman. I trust her completely. She was brilliant when we lost our precious Amy five years ago. She helped me to keep my sanity, you know. I was so bloody stoic in front of you, supporting you in our loss. It was Angela who noticed that I wasn't really coping at all. She popped in and delivered me some home-made soup and food when you were recovering from your hysterectomy in hospital."

"Oliver, why didn't you tell me about this before?"

"Simply because I love you, my love, and you were the last person in the world that I wanted to upset more than you were already at that time." He grinned at her, and then gave her a long, lingering kiss. "Now Jane Doe, off you go to deliver Harry to his new owner."

An hour later, Jane parked her car outside the Summer's home. *Well, Harry, you'll be with Jenny and her Pooh Bear and more importantly, with your Vicki's heart!* She took a deep breath, gave Harry a big hug, as promised to Vicki, and then got out of her car. She tucked Harry under one arm and walked up the path to the front door and rang the bell. She grinned at Harry, who was sporting a neat pale blue bow tie, which she had bought down the street in Gisborne, before she drove south.

Jenny's mother answered the door.

"Hello, you must be Detective Chief Superintendent Jane Doe. Please come in." She then whispered to Jane, "I haven't told Jenny what you were bringing today. My husband and I think it's a wonderful gift from the donor's family...as if they haven't given us enough already! By the way, my husband apologises for not being here, but he had to go to work."

Jane was ushered inside to the lounge room. Jenny's mother sat next to her daughter. Jenny's eyes lit up.

"Hello, Jane. A teddy? For me? Why?"

"Jenny, his name is Harry, and he's a special teddy bear who wants to sit next to your Pooh Bear in your bedroom, and be his buddy."

"Why is Harry so special?" Jenny took Harry and cuddled him. "Hey, he's cute!"

"Harry belonged to a girl, the same age as you. His owner died, and her parents consented to her organs to be donated to several people..."

"Cool! So he used to belong to my donor's heart? I mean, he belonged to my donor?"

"Absolutely! Her parents wanted you to have Harry, so he could be near to his former owner. He looked so sad without her."

Jenny hugged Harry again. "Hello, Harry. Come on Harry, I want you to meet Pooh... Oops! Sorry..." She turned to Jane. "Thanks for bringing him to me. I know you can't tell me who they are, but could you thank them for me?"

"I will." Jane got up. "I must get to work, myself, now. See you sometime, Jenny."

Jenny looked at her and said, "I hope so. I'd like to see Oliver too, sometime. He helped to stop my nightmares...he's terrific! And so are you... I didn't know you were a policewoman. Mum told me that you learnt psychology at Uni, like Oliver. I want to be a psychologist when I grow up...or maybe a clever policewoman, like you." With those words, Jenny left the room, holding her new friend.

Jane said, "I must go now, I've got lots to do today."

"Of course. Thank you for bringing such a precious gift, Jane Doe. You're a special person."

Jane left and drove south to the St. Kilda Police complex. After parking her car, she went straight up to her office. *The best part of my job, I'm glad to be back at the pointy end!*

Stan and Angela were busy at their desks when Jane arrived. Fred was also there, sporting a lovely blue cravat. He looked up at her and said, "Morning, lovely lady. We have received some good news whilst you were delivering that special gift to Jenny."

"Oh, what's the news?"

Stan and Angela got up from their desks, holding some official papers.

Stan said, "The Department of Public Prosecution has given our squad a glowing report on our case file."

Angela added, "And they've managed to get a hearing this afternoon at the Melbourne Central Magistrates Court, to accept the evidence and charge Graham Pappas/Polites. Yes, they are using both names, because, like us, they are sure the deed poll name change isn't legal, and they don't want any hitches when charging Graham. Oh, and Graham still doesn't want a solicitor. He's representing himself...and most importantly...is pleading guilty!"

Jane grinned. "Hurray! That will save the courts lots of money. I presume he'll be remanded in custody until a future date is fixed for sentencing?"

Angela replied, "Got it in one, Boss. The DPP don't want him bailed. Also, the Pappas family don't want to offer bail money for him."

Jane retorted, "So he's lost the support of his adopted family, too. He's going to have a very lonely life in the future. What a stupid man!"

Fred got up. "Well, I've also heard on the grapevine that the Special Cold Case Squad have received a pile of new cases to solve. So it looks like we'd all better enjoy our weekend off, and get ready for more delving into the past."

Jane nodded, "Yes, the Assistant Commissioner contacted me yesterday late afternoon, and told me about the new cases. He's put them in order of priority. So we won't be out of work for months and months. For now, I think, we'd all better recheck our paperwork to make sure everything is in order, just in case the DPP calls us for extra information if it's needed in the court this afternoon."

"Are we all attending the hearing this afternoon, Boss?" asked Angela.

"Yes, why not. It's our first case, and it's been rather special, hasn't it?"

At one thirty that afternoon, the members of the Special Cold Case Squad attended the hearing. Graham Pappas/Polites sat stony-faced, staring straight ahead at the Senior Magistrate. When he was asked how he wished to plead to the charges before the court, Graham quietly said, "Guilty, Sir."

Jane breathed a sigh of relief.

Yes! We've finally got him in custody!

She also noticed the smiles on her colleagues' faces as the Magistrate told Graham that he would not be bailed, and that he was going to be held in custody until a date was fixed at the Court for his sentencing.

Graham was then led away handcuffed, to be taken back to the Central Remand Centre.

Outside, the Cold Case team finally rejoiced.

"Yes!" said Jane.

"At last!" added Angela.

"He'll get what he bloody deserves!" growled Stan.

Fred, kissed the back of Jane's hand, and said, "Congratulations, lovely lady. It's a pleasure to work with you!"

They returned to the police complex. Jane sat with them for half an hour and showed them the new cases that were now ready for them to explore the following week.

"We don't really have to do them one by one. In fact we might find that we could cope with more than one at a time."

"We'll need more staff, Boss," said Stan.

Angela looked straight a Jane with a small smile.

Jane looked at Stan. "Well, that's up to our Assistant Commissioner. We'll see. Now, I think it's time for us to clear up our desks ready for next week."

"But it's only four o'clock!" exclaimed Angela.

"I know, everyone, but I'm sending you all home early for the weekend," responded Jane, and then added, "Now get organised and go before I change my mind," she grinned.

Ten minutes later, the office was empty. Jane was left alone to ponder upon what had happened during the last week.

What a great team. Heck, the expression on Angel's face was classic when Stan said we needed more staff. Fingers crossed Steve will say yes to my offer when they come for lunch on Sunday. I need him for all this workload that we've got!

She sighed, and then finally closed the office to drive north to Gisborne.

Oliver greeted her at the front door with Sassy and Spunky, the dogs jumping up at her, wagging their tails.

"By the look on your face, you've had a very successful day," said Oliver. "I have to confess, though, that tonight I haven't cooked dinner."

"Oh? Well, I'll help you now, if you like..."

"No, don't bother, my love. I've already bought some lovely fish and chips from down the village. It's being kept warm in the oven."

"Ooh yum, that sounds perfect. Let's eat now, I'm hungry."

They sat contentedly, leaving some crunchy chips to the last, to eat in their fingers, by the open fire. When they finished, they sat together, sipping hot coffee, and chatted about the events of the last week. The clock chimed nine times.

"Oliver, let's clean up."

"Okay, screw up the paper and we'll put it in the bin. Hey, it's easier than washing dishes!"

In the kitchen, Oliver turned to Jane and asked, "Did Jenny like Harry?"

"It was love at first sight. The last time I saw Jenny, she was rushing down the hall to her room to introduce Harry to Pooh Bear. Mind you, she also thanked me and the donor for her lovely gift. She's quite a delightful, natural girl."

"So it's a happy ending of sorts?"

"Yes, Oliver, in that regard it has been."

"It's also good to hear that Graham has pleaded guilty. I wonder what length of sentence he'll get."

"Goodness knows...that's up to the courts to decide. At least he's been caught...that's our job done." Jane stopped for a moment and added, "Oh, I told the squad about you and me knowing Vicki's recipient..."

"What?"

"Only the facts, Oliver. I said that the recipient was a patient of yours, and that she was having nightmares about being murdered, shortly after receiving a new heart. Your patient was describing the house that belonged to Vicki! And that's when you let me know that information to possibly help in the investigation. So my team only know that we were working on facts received and backed up by research studies of donor recipients experiencing things that only the original owner of the organ knew. I must admit it was a bit spooky though, when Angel said she had a good sub title for the case file...*Haunted Heart*. My heart nearly missed a beat when she suggested that name!"

"I bet! Just as well you only stuck to the facts, my love. Talking about haunted hearts... I presume you've mentioned seeing a ghost again to Steve?"

"Yes, I did tell him, shortly after I first saw her in the bedroom that day. Steve was thrilled that my supernatural powers have returned, of course. Mind you, I still suspect that Angel knows--even if only by instinct--hence using the name *Haunted Heart*. What do you think?"

"Yes, maybe she does...but she'll keep it to herself. I don't think she'll say anything to Steve, even when and if they are working together...which I hope they will. What an addition to your team!"

"Steve should let me know his decision on Sunday. I'm looking forward to seeing them all again. The kids are lovely...a credit to their parents."

"I've defrosted the sausages this morning. Kids love sausage sizzles. I'm sure the adults will enjoy them too." Jane yawned. Oliver added, "You look tired, Jane. Are you okay?"

"Yes, I'm fine. I think the last couple of days have been fairly emotional, to say the least. Talking to ghosts always seems to affect me like this... it's a weird experience, but not entirely unpleasant."

"Well, I think we should have an early night. Tomorrow we can enjoy a quiet day on our little farm, and get ready for the Ho family visit."

Jane yawned again and then stretched. "What a good idea. I could sleep for a week!"

Epilogue

On Sunday, as planned, the Ho family arrived sharp at eleven in the morning at *Wyndales*.

Spunky and Sassy gave them a warm welcome first, as their human mum and dad, Jane and Oliver, as usual, weren't fast enough out of the front door.

Jane gave everyone a kiss. "Hello everyone!" She looked at Kylie and Khan. "Gosh, you two have grown another couple of centimetres since we last saw you. Khan, you're getting more handsome each day, just like your dad, and Kylie, you're very pretty, like your mum." The children giggled and hugged Jane. "Hey, you two, you're both starting to squeeze me too tight...I need to breathe." She laughed as the five year old twins giggled and let her go.

Kylie asked, "Auntie Jane, Uncle Oliver, can we play with Sassy and Spunky in the back paddock for a while?"

Khan rushed up to Jane and tugged her arm. "And can we go out later and pat the Alpacas?"

Oliver smiled at them and said, "Of course you can. There's plenty of time for us to all go out and pat the Alpacas before we have our sausage sizzle."

Kylie and Khan yelled with delight. Khan grabbed his sister's hand and said, "Thank you, Uncle Oliver. Come on, Sassy and Spunky...let's go play!" The children ran through the house, with the two excited dogs following them. They went through the kitchen, out the back door and into the rabbit-proofed, fenced off small paddock, which had been closely mowed, to prevent snakes coming too near to the homestead.

Half an hour later, Jane, Oliver, Steve, Angel, Kylie and Khan followed the now slightly weary dogs out to the larger paddock to pat the Alpaca herd.

Khan looked at his father. "Daddy, can we get an Alpaca as a pet?"

Steve smiled at his son. "It would be nice, but these guys are pack animals, and only having one would make it lonely and sad. Besides, our suburban back yard is too small...but not too small for a puppy."

Khan replied, "Wow, a puppy...can we get one tomorrow?"

Angela remarked, "Well, not that quickly...remember puppies need lots of looking after and training and walking each day. I think we could wait for the next long school holidays..."

Jane beckoned Angela across to her and talked quietly into her ear, "We were going to tell you later...but I guess we could tell my two favourite children at lunch...." Jane whispered something into Angela's ear, so no one else could hear.

Angela grinned, "Terrific!"

Jane smiled, "Okay, let's all go back and get ready for the sausage sizzle. I have something to tell you at lunch."

Everyone was seated around the outdoor garden table setting under the large verandah.

Kylie was wide eyed when she asked, "Auntie Jane, what's the exciting news?"

Jane winked at Angela. "Oh, I nearly forgot. Sorry, just teasing!" she laughed, "You know that Spunky is a boy dog and Sassy is a girl dog?"

Khan replied, "Of course we do."

Jane leaned forward, her elbows on the rustic table. "We found out at the vet a few weeks ago that Sassy is pregnant. Would you like to have the *pick of the litter?*"

Kylie frowned and asked, "What does that mean, Auntie Jane?"

Jane responded, "It means the best puppy in the litter."

Khan pointed to his chest and said, "Cool... I want a boy dog."

Kylie said, "I want a girl dog..."

Jane smiled at them. "Why don't we give you two puppies, a boy and a girl?"

Kylie grinned and added, "Yeah, they can have puppies too."

Jane reacted, "Um no, not really, not a brother and sister. You see, Sassy and Spunky are not related. We adopted them, hoping that they might have puppies...and that is what happened."

Khan nodded at Jane. "We can neuter our puppies!"

Steve, eyes wide, asked, "Where did you learn about that, Khan?"

"In the newspaper. The R.S.P.C.A. wants to neuter cats, and dogs. I looked in my dictionary. I know what it means."

Oliver remarked, "My, I knew you loved to read, Khan, but it looks like you're going to be quite a scholar."

Kylie asked, "Can we visit here soon and give Sassy a pat and see how her puppies are growing inside her?"

Steve's eyes nearly popped out of his head. "I didn't know you knew about puppies!" he grinned. "Boy, I obviously led a sheltered childhood in Hong Kong!"

Once lunch was finished, the children went inside to the den with the two sleepy dogs. Kahn sat and read a train book, while Kylie played with her Barbie doll.

The four adults sat in the lounge room for the next hour and chatted about the two cases.

Oliver asked, "Who's driving home?"

Angela replied, "Obviously, it's me, because I haven't been drinking. I will when we get home, though."

Oliver said, "I only asked because I'll pour a little bubbly for three of us, and a mineral water for you, Angel." He poured the drinks and brought them to the coffee table on a tray. "I'd like to propose a toast to the Special Crime Squad, and to the new Special Cold Case Squad, for two difficult cases solved...well done!"

Jane, Steve, Angela and Oliver, raised their glasses and chorused, "Cheers!"

Steve smiled, and said, "Thanks for the toast, Oliver. I wish to make another toast...to Jane, a special lady I've worked with in the Special Crime Squad five years ago...and a lady whom I've worked in conjunction with on both our cases, because they were linked." He raised his glass. "Here's to you and the future, Boss."

Jane blushed, "Thank you, Steve, as you keep reminding me...it's a pleasure to work with you again."

Steve replied, "Yes, Boss, it will be again too," he grinned and put an arm around Angela, "because last night, after a short chat with Angel, I made a decision to say *yes* to your kind offer, and join your squad!"

Jane got up and hugged Steve, "That's great news, Steve." She turned to Angela, "It will be an even stronger squad. I'll tell the Assistant Commissioner first thing tomorrow morning. I know he's keen to get Sergeant Jason Standing moved across to replace you, Steve."

"What a week it's been, Boss," remarked Angela. She raised her mineral water and added, "Here's to the Special Cold Case Squad!"

"Cheers!"

Postscript

I based this mystery on a true story, told to me by a Senior Pathologist in the UK, during a stay with hubby, Dave at the famous Cley Windmill near Holt, Norfolk in 2001.

Dave told him I was a mystery writer, who added a dimension of paranormal to the plot. To my astonishment, he told us that he didn't laugh about the paranormal after a unique experience doing a second post mortem on a young girl, for a police Superintendent friend.

He proved that the child had been murdered, and her death was not an accident. He then found out that a second child, who had received the dead child's heart, was having nightmares, and had been describing the death scene in detail! It was a house and town that she had never visited.

Guess who was awake that night, setting up the plot for my next Jane Doe mystery?

At the time, Dave & I knew that one day, due to genetic kidney disease, he would have to have dialysis and/or a kidney transplant.

The spooky part of *Haunted Heart* for me personally, is that little did I know, ten years later I would donate one of my kidneys to Dave...with 98% compatibility!

I dedicate this book to the Royal Melbourne Hospital Renal Transplant Unit.

If you enjoyed this author's book, then please place a review up at the site of purchase, and any social media sites you frequent!

can find ALL our books up on our website at:

http://www.writers-exchange.com

All Wendy's books:

http://www.writers-exchange.com/Wendy-Laing/

All our Mystery/Thriller books:

https://www.writers-exchange.com/category/genres/mystery-thrillers-suspense/

About the Author

Wendy Laing is one half of the pseudonym or pen name "Dalziel Laing" of Dianne Dalziel and Wendy Laing, the co-authors of *Mirror, Mirror.* She is also a multi-published author in her own right.

In retirement, a writer, with a Teaching Diploma, a Bachelor of Arts Degree with majors in professional Writing (creative writing editing, publishing and Journalism) and Communications (mass media, and gender imaging) with electives in Literary Studies and Sociology, and Master of Arts (project/thesis called: "Severance Packages, A crime/Paranormal Novel and Exegesis focussing on the electronic and Digital publication of Creative Writing".

A "Jill-Of-All-Trades" Teacher, curriculum consultant, travel consultant, International Airline employee in passenger and cargo areas at Melbourne International Airport and city offices, and a Professional Dog Trainer! Wendy's had articles published in *The Sunbury Times* and *The Anthony Warlow International Newsletter.*

Member of the FAW (Fellowship of Australian Writers)

Member of the VWC (Victorian Writers Centre)

Lifetime Alumni of Victoria University

Member of Sister in Crime

Widowed in 2016, Wendy lives in a retirement village with her four pawed family, Vicky, a sooky & loving adopted black Greyhound, whom she has trained and takes to Pet therapy at the local aged care each week - a hobby that she has enjoyed for over 30 years.

Keep track of Wendy's many books on her author page:

http://www.writers-exchange.com/Wendy-Laing/

If you want to read more about books by this author, they are listed on the following pages...

Captain Angus, the Lighthouse Ghost

{Mid-Grade Reader: Paranormal}

Two children holidaying at the Cape Otway Lighthouse Station in Victoria Australia meet the ghost of an old Scottish sea captain who roams the world helping the 'spirits' of lighthouses and helping 'conserve' the towers. Captain Angus befriends the children and takes them on virtual reality trips via a magic time tunnel. Together, they experience sailing on an old sailor's vessel, see a shipwreck rescue, witness the tower being built, and even meet one of their own ancestors!

Publisher: http://www.writers-exchange.com/captain-angus-the-lighthouse-ghost/

Cock of the Walk

{Murder Mystery}

When Sir Peter Percival, owner of the Woodburne Wine Estate and former member of Parliament, is found dead, three Australian detectives embark on a baffling investigation in which it appears *everyone* has a motive...

Publisher: http://www.writers-exchange.com/cock-of-the-walk/

Jane Doe Mystery Series

{Mystery/Paranormal}

As the daughter of a policeman who died in the line of duty, Inspector Jane Doe, head of Melbourne Homicide, is single-mindedly driven to seek justice for all. But Jane is no ordinary detective. She can communicate with the ghosts of murder victims. Not wanting to be dismissed as mentally unstable, she must keep her secret from all but her husband and her senior officer, using each victim's information to subtly direct her team in the right direction on each case. Jane realizes she's the only thing standing between a killer being brought to justice and a monster getting off scot-free. But, with each case she solves, her fear that the police hierarchy will accidentally discover her secret forces her to walk a fine line indeed.

Book 1: Flowers from the Grave

Recovering from near fatal head injuries received from a serial killer, who is still at large, Inspector Jane Doe, head of Melbourne Homicide, is staying in an isolated clifftop cottage. Ryan, a stranger on the beach, befriends her. But Jane's idyllic sojourn turns into a nightmare. Flowers arrive with threatening notes attached. Worse, she can't help but believe that Ryan is some kind of ghost, and, if he is, is he friend or foe? Has the serial killer she apprehended in the name of justice returned to finish what he started and make her his next victim?

Publisher: http://www.writers-exchange.com/flowers-from-the-grave/

Book 2: Severance Packages

Set in the peaceful town of Sunbury, Australia, Inspector Jane Doe, head of Melbourne Homicide, once again deals with a serial killer after grisly, dismembered body parts are discovered at a local winery and the rubbish dump. Jane has to act fast to stop any more of these 'severance packages' from being delivered.

Publisher: http://www.writers-exchange.com/severance-packages/

Book 3: Haunted Heart

Head of Melbourne Homicide, Inspector Jane Doe's first Cold Case involves the recent death of a daughter of a Member of Parliament. After he disagrees with the first coroner's verdict of accidental death, the MP secures a second autopsy that reveals his daughter was murdered. At the same time, Jane's husband Oliver is dealing with a young heart transplant recipient who's having nightmares of being murdered. Elsewhere, another law enforcement officer, Steve Ho, investigates the murder of an eminent heart transplant surgeon found in a local lake. Jane, Oliver and Steve become embroiled in a case that will surely haunt them all for years to come.

Publisher: http://www.writers-exchange.com/Haunted-Heart/

Book 4: Cadavers' Cave

Chief Superintendent of the Cold Case Squad, Jane Doe has a formidable list of special, unsolved cases littering her desk. Taking a break is a luxury she doesn't often allow herself. However, during a rare weekend off, she catches a news story involving a dead body wrapped in a plastic shroud. The gruesome discovery was made in the cliffs below the Point Lonsdale Lighthouse--directly near the entrance to the Port Phillip Bay in Victoria, Australia. Rough winter weather combined with unusually heavy, high tides washed away the grave, leaving it partially covered in rocks and seaweed. The coroner estimates that the body had been buried there for at least a year. The last thing Jane needs is another case to hit her already groaning desk, but something eerie took place in Cadavers' Cave and she may be the only one who can solve a mystery equally troubling and tragic.

Publisher: http://www.writers-exchange.com/Cadavers-Cave/

Book 5: The Ghostly Gum

Detective Chief Superintendent Jane Doe has a formidable list of cold cases on her desk. This latest one involves an unidentified person, murdered seventeen years earlier.

It is not only a perplexing case, but also an exploratory challenge for all involved as the squad try not only to identify the victim, but sort out suspects who are involved in money laundering, drugs and family feuds.

Jane's team are challenged to find solid forensic proof to use against the main suspect, so he doesn't get away with a cold-blooded murder.

Publisher: http://www.writers-exchange.com/The-Ghostly-Gum/

Mind's Eye-The imagery of remembered scenes
{Poetry}

A collection of poems encompassing one life filled with images from childhood, family, pets, the Australian countryside around, and delivered with a touch of homespun philosophy.

Publisher: http://www.writers-exchange.com/Minds-Eye/

Mirror, Mirror
with Di Dalziel (writing as Dalziel Laing)
{Murder Mystery}

Inspector Georgina Borg's life is an emotional rollercoaster. She's deeply in love with Professor Richard Thompson yet can't get herself to commit to a permanent relationship--a puzzle even she can't explain adequately. At work, she's in charge of a case pursuing a serial killer who's remained a mystery for ten long years. She's followed his distinctive but maddeningly elusive trail from Sydney to Melbourne. Now suddenly the killer targets a victim with an entirely new profile. Despite the change in modus operandi, Borg is certain it's the same killer. Just when she thinks she's close to solving the puzzle and revealing his identity at last, her should-be, would-be fiancé becomes the prime suspect!

Publisher: http://www.writers-exchange.com/Mirror-Mirror/

Sir Henry, the Knight in Space

{Science Fiction/Mid-Grade Reader}

Twin boys accidentally beam the ghost of 14th century Sir Henry de Bohun into their father's spaceship in 3000 AD. Let the fun begin as they take a virtual trip back in time to visit Sir Henry's English castle!

Publisher: http://www.writers-exchange.com/Sir-Henry-the-Knight-In-Space/

Tarmac Tales
By Wendy and Dave Laing

In this fact-based collection of experiences in the airline and travel industries gathered by authors with a combined fifty-two years working in all capacities of the business, you'll be given a behind-the-scenes look at the inner operations of this sometimes funny, sometimes sad, but always entertaining trade.

Publisher: http://www.writers-exchange.com/Tarmac-Tales/

Under the Coolabah Tree

{A Collection of Australian Poetry}

Fun, amusing, sometimes rowdy and always delightfully full of Australian colour, this collection of Australian Bush poems is best read out loud--if you dare to try an Aussie accent!

Publisher: http://www.writers-exchange.com/Under-the-Coolabah-Tree/

You can find ALL our books on our website at:

http://www.writers-exchange.com

All Wendy's books:

http://www.writers-exchange.com/Wendy-Laing/

All our Mystery/Thriller books:

https://www.writers-exchange.com/category/genres/mystery-thrillers-suspense/